WE ARE PLAYING ROULETTE WITH YOUR FUTURE

LESSONS OF A POST-WAR, HIPPIE-SYMPATHIZING, ECO-FRIENDLY ENTREPRENEUR

G. SPENCER MYERS

Creator of the Dr. Derk Bryan Eco-Thriller Series

Other Books by G. Spencer Myers

Pest:

A man experiences a deadly premonition while fishing in the Florida Keys. A murder in Michigan causes a toxic spill. Dr. Derk Bryan, the Indiana Jones of the EPA, soon discovers that these two disparate events threaten every drop of water on the planet and every important relationship in his life. His laisse faire life on the beach is on a collision course with the maniacal chemical company magnate, Jack Von Lleuwan, and his bodyguard, Jimmy "Gloves Swingle, an ex-wrestler with anger management issues.

Von Lleuwan's newest product, PESTfree© , designed to replace the chemicals that are contaminating food and water worldwide, contains a deadly flaw. As a result, Kate McCardigan, Derk's college sweetheart, becomes a target when she blames Von Lleuwan for crippling her son and others. As the body count grows, Derk Bryan races against the clock to thwart disaster and save McCardigan from becoming another victim.

Praise for Pest:

"Murder leads Derk Bryan, the EPA's most creative investigator, from a chemical spill in West Michigan to Tampa Bay and back to Ohio. Pest will make you laugh and make you cry. Ultimately, you will ask, Will I be the next victim? A must-read book."

- **Ervin Harmon, Book Reviewer, and Critic**

"The engaging narrative of Pest contains much to think about regarding toxicology, environmental awareness, and the balance of nature. . . Pest leaves one wondering how closely the story resembles a true one."

- **Rachel Elaine, Author of Thoughts for Thought.**

Dead Wrong:

A truckload of toxic chemicals crashes into Tampa Bay, a bank president's son and a senator's daughter die after smoking weed at a fraternity party, and the publisher of a weekly entertainment rag accuses the cops of murder. As one of the EPA's top investigators, Derk Bryan refuses to accept the ME's conclusion that the spill was an accident and that these events are not related. With three monster hurricanes on a collision course with Florida, Bryan races against the clock and the bureaucracy to uncover the clues in this ecological crossword puzzle.

Praise for Dead Wrong:

"Using an EPA investigator is unique for a crime novel. I really like Derk Bryan and I really liked this book."

- **Ann Bocock WXEL-TV, "Between the Sheets" Summer Reading Series.**

"Dr. Derk Bryan is a hero without a Messiah complex."

- **Buch 1-DM, Online Book Club**

"Impressive characters headline this suspenseful tale with an ecological bent."

- **Kirkus review**

". . . interesting, thought-provoking, and thrilling . . . There is no doubt that audiences will be anticipating the next adventure."

- **Gretchen Hansen, The US Review of Books**

The Girl with the Red Nails:

In The Girl with the Red Nails, Dr. Derk Bryan, the Indiana Jones of the EPA, pursues the greedy and the complicit who are fueling an approaching catastrophe.

All roads lead to the doorstep of Pendleton Danswirth III and his billionaire buddies. It looks as if he'll get away with murder and more until an ending that no one saw coming.

Greed, sex, religion and murder drive this eco-thriller. A must read!

We Are Playing Roulette With Your Future:

G. Spencer Myers issues a profound warning to Ian, his grandson, and Ian's generation that involves a threat to humanity so great that scientists have given it a name: The Anthropocene—a human caused extinction.

Using a series of short stories Myers challenges grandsons from eight to eighty to think big and be bold in your ideas in the face of the crisis of your lifetime: Global Warming. In 1980, he became the first person in the U.S. to put 400 sq. ft. of solar panels on a multi-family residence listed on the National Register of Historic Places. Today, he drives an EV and fuels it with sunshine. Having devoted his life to reducing his own carbon footprint, he says, "There's hope. We know what to do." Read it and become inspired.

All books are available at: www.GSpencerMyers.com or your favorite online book provider.

Dedicated to All Grandchildren

It has been seven years since I gave my grandson, Ian, the first edition of this book entitled, A Letter to My Grandson. It was intended as an introduction to your family accompanied by a feeble attempt to offer some grandfatherly wisdom that you might find relevant to your own life. Looking back, at age ten, I should have realized that you probably preferred a new bicycle or a computer game. The teacher in me prevailed and, somehow a theme coursed its way through this book until it became the inspiration for the 1st Palm Beach County Short Story Contest entitled In Search of Integrity. That was 2017. A lot has happened since then. It affects everyone. It's not good. And, you're not going to like it.

While you have grown into a gifted young man with a keen sense of humor, an interest in math and engineering and a love of lacrosse, I have written two more Dr. Derk Bryan ecological thrillers. My golf game suffered the loss of two club lengths in distance after recuperating from surgery while you took a parttime job, got a license to drive and became big enough and smart enough to beat me in basketball and chess. I lost 20lbs while you grew three feet.

During that same seven years, we, the people of Earth, have spewed out one fourth of all of the greenhouse gases humans have emitted since the beginning of the industrial revolution, circa 1750.

Why is this be important to you? These pollutants, created by burning the stuff that has powered our cars, home and businesses, have been accumulating in our atmosphere for two hundred and fifty years causing the temperature on Earth to rise. If we continue on this self-destructive path the Earth will heat up to levels not experienced for 38 million years.

Scientists, such as you aspire to be, tell us that life, as we know it, is not possible at these temperatures.

Now that I have your attention, I apologize. You didn't expect to face this kind of challenge. It didn't have to happen, and it's not fair. At a time when you should be focusing upon football and lacrosse practice, jobs, friends, music and getting a date, you should not be responsible for saving the world from a life-threatening crisis. As Al Gore, the former Vice President, warned us in his book and documentary twenty years ago, "Whether you call it Climate Change, Global Warming or The Sixth Extinction, we must stop over-heating our planet. There is no plan B."

Since you will live your entire life engaged with this enemy I am dedicating this new edition to all grandchildren. In WE ARE PLAYING ROULETTE WITH YOUR FUTURE, I'll tell you some humorous stories about our family . . . they were an entertaining bunch . . . a few lessons I learned about life and how I came to understand the profound threat that global warming presents to you and all grandchildren. In this new version I have asked you to share your thoughts as you approach the time in your life when every decision you make will either feed or defeat this enemy. Thank goodness, we know what to do.

You have my apology for leaving you the world in this condition, and I know it's easy to blame those of us whom came before you, but keep this in mind. You are not obligated by your ancestors' actions, only burdened by their mistakes. You are free to develop your own path forward. Collectively, your generation, unified in purpose, can build models for a brighter future. The world, troubled as it is, can be your oyster. This is not a gloom or doom situation because we know what to do.

I begin with this question: what exactly is this crisis? You have probably read or heard about climate change. It's a euphemistic term to describe what is occurring. Our homes are like greenhouses in that they become really hot when the sunshine enters them. Likewise, if you go into your home, lock it and seal all of the windows and doors and light a fire, the temperature in your home will rise until nothing can survive. This is exactly what is happening on Earth, our planetary home.

How did this happen? In short, the way we fuel our cars, heat and cool our homes, power our businesses and grow our food is producing pollution in the form of greenhouse gas (GHG) that is collecting in our atmosphere and warming our planet. This is creating a recipe for disaster that scientists are calling the Anthropocene Age --- in other words, The Sixth Extinction, this time a human caused extinction.

Could this actually happen on Earth? Could we or any other life form be wiped off the planet? Yes. There have been five other times when all or most of the life on the planet was eliminated. The most recent one occurred 65 million years ago and is known for killing the dinosaurs like the ones you see in museums and the Jurassic Park movies.

Earlier I said that you wouldn't like what is happening, but the truth is we cannot continue down this road much longer. Fortunately, this is not a problem of science. It's a matter of human will. We know what we have to do. Are you, am I, is anyone willing to evolve? If we get this right the future can be much healthier, more exotic and less violent.

I said we know what to do. I'm referring to the teams of scientists, engineers, educators and journalists who have devoted years to identifying and providing solutions. This threat to humanity is occurring in spite of constant reminders by scientists since the late 1970s. We have talked a lot about this crisis, but our accomplishment thus far are far from adequate. Our denials and delays have resulted in worldwide fires, floods, droughts, hurricanes, mass migrations, cultural clashes and violence. Scenes of the dead and the damage appear on our phones and televisions endlessly.

The people of Chicago and Detroit are forced to wear masks to filter the smoke from forest fires in Oregon. The streets of coastal cities from Miami to New Jersey are flooded from the rising seas as a result of melting glaciers in Greenland. Storms are more frequent and stronger than ever before. Neighborhoods and small towns are being incinerated or washed away. The risks and the costs are escalating. Four decades ago, there was a weather-related event once every three months that caused over one billion dollars of damage. Today that occurs almost twice each month.

Our ecosystems are breaking down. Let's take a look at the impact upon just one of them: oceans.

- Oceans cover 70% of our planet. Healthy oceans are necessary for our food supply and to absorb the carbon dioxide (CO2) from burning fossil fuels. Global warming is making the oceans more acidic. Normal has been 8.2Ph. We're on course for 7.8Ph. This drop seems like a small change, but most of the life in the ocean will not have time to adapt to this change. Changes of this magnitude usually occur over thousands or hundreds of thousands of years. With the Ph levels changing so rapidly the oceans will not be able to provide the food we need or trap enough greenhouse gas to save us.
- By burning fossil fuels, we are raising the temperature on Earth so much that polar caps and glaciers throughout the world are melting. Fifty percent of the Arctic Sea ice has melted in the past 30 years. It's like dropping ice cubes into a full glass of water. When the ice melts sea levels rise all over the world and flood coastal communities. When Twait's Glacier, a block of ice the size of Florida on the west coast of Antarctica, drops into the sea, as is inevitable if we maintain the course, water levels will rise from 8-16 feet all over the world. My own home in Florida will be under water. Forty percent of the population

lives with 40 miles of a coastline. Goodbye to homes and businesses worldwide.

When I was seventeen. I was eager to become an adult and, other than nuclear war, there was no other threat to my prosperity and longevity. I can't say that about your future. If we stay on this course, by 2070, one of three inhabitants of Earth could be residing on lands that cannot sustain life. For today's teenagers, that is less than fifty years from now.

I am not a scientist so how did I become aware of this problem? I grew up in a small town surrounded by farms and wildlife. I enjoyed hiking through the woods, fishing and hunting for small game and swimming in the ponds and lakes that were within bicycle distance. While sitting in a row boat on a lake about fifteen miles from Battle Creek, Michigan, I got my first lesson in ecology while fishing with my grandfather. The fishing was terrible. When I did catch one, it was too small to keep. Grandpa said this was because the people living next to the lake had faulty septic systems, buried their trash in the ground and discarded the oil from their cars directly onto the soil. "These pollutants wash into water, contaminate the wildlife and are destroying the entire lake," he said.

Over the years, I watched the things my grandfather described contaminate water all over the world. It's so prevalent that the Environmental Protection Agency recently informed us that there are microparticles of plastic in our drinking water. Accounts of these pollutants building up in our air, water and soil caused me to change my own habits and to create the Dr. Derk Brayn ecological thriller series as a means to educate and entertain others. It was my grandfather who first alerted me to what has become a crisis. My hope is that I can inspire you to confront and conquer this enemy before it overcomes us.

At seventeen, forty-six years may seem like a long time. It's not in climate years but this is the salient point. According to climate experts, the tipping point for ecological disaster --- the point from which there is no return --- will occur when we have increased the global temperature 2.0 degrees Centigrade (3.6 degrees F) above pre-industrial times. That doesn't seem like much, but we are approaching that point so rapidly that scientists have essentially resigned themselves to this event. Therefore, neither you nor any of today's teenagers has forty-six, thirty-five or even twenty years to slow down this runaway train.

Is this disaster inevitable? NO! We know what to do.

Before I get to that you should be aware of one more thing. Part of the problem you and your generation are facing is the result of expectations we have imposed upon you. We conditioned you to expect to achieve a lofty standard of living in the same way we did, by over producing and over consuming, by creating wealth and abundance fueled by oil, coal and gas --- the very things that are threatening our lives. We are going to have to develop a different way of measuring well-being in the future. We cannot keep buying trinkets and throwing them away after the whim has passed. We are going to have to stop using gas and oil to power our cars, our homes and our offices. We must create an economy that values education, health, art, relationships and human activities that are not based upon material consumption --- certainly not consumption that is burying us in our own waste. We must strive to reduce the exploitation of people and our natural resources in ways that does not disenfranchise so many or choke us to death on the exhaust.

There is no way to sugar coat this challenge. The future is grim if you continue on the roads we have paved for you.

Why do I say there is hope? Humans are a miraculously gifted species. What separates us from other species is our ability to imagine things that do not currently exist. During my grandfather's lifetime, he witnessed the development of a national highway system, air travel, the telephone, the television and atomic energy. He was part of a generation that overcame two world wars, instituted social security, unemployment compensation, Medicare and sent men into space. These were big ideas that required national, sometimes global, efforts. All hands-on board. Everyone had to participate. His generation proved that together we can create great things.

During my time on Earth, we developed the computer chip, the Internet and formed the United Nations which gave rise to the Intergovernmental Panel on Climate Change (IPCC). This enables all nations to gather together in an effort to overcome this crisis. My generation increased the standard of living for millions of people. Unfortunately, unlike the achievements during my grandfather's life, our modus operandi has been every man for himself. Although the Internet has assisted mankind in many ways, the increases in the standard of living came mostly for those with access to fossil fuels and at the expense of many whose labor and natural resources were being exploited. The enormous gap between the poor and the wealthy that this created has not been healthy for our environment. It will be up to you fashion a world that overcomes the failures of the old models and creates a brighter, more sustainable future. I believe you can do it.

I have said that we know what to do. In simplest terms this means that you, in fact, all of us, will have to reduce the use of pesticides, plastics and fossil fuels. They have become an addiction for us, and addictions don't usually have happy endings. At least, to a large degree, the solution is in your hands. Change your own habits, and the world will change, too. It will be much easier to get businesses and governments to amend their behaviors, as well.

This will not be easy because half the citizens of Earth have benefited from the creation of this crisis, including many reading this book. They will be reluctant to change until there are models of behavior available to them. That's why it is imperative that you make brave new choices, become leaders.

One of the delightful aspects of youth is that you're not burdened by the attitudes of your ancestors, only their mistakes. You are free to plot your own course. Another trait associated with youth is idealism. My generation strived to overcome racism and sexism, two lofty ideals, not yet fully realized. You can and must travel a new path that offers a new destination for mankind. One that will probably challenge the fundamental mindset of our institutions and our economic models. One that places the outcomes of people's well-being on this planet on the same plateau as profit. Certainly, one that is not dependent upon fossil fuels. It will require the participation of almost everyone, particularly those whom have benefitted the most from the models that encouraged exploitation without regard to the outcomes for others not so fortunate. Somehow, you'll have to convince the wealthiest ten percent, who are responsible for 50% of the global greenhouse gas emissions, to participate with you. It will not be easy, but to paraphrase former President John F. Kennedy, "You will do it because it is hard," and because your own well-being will depend upon it.

I have said we know what to do because scientists tell us that. Here are some obvious places to begin. Utility companies are responsible for 25% of greenhouse gas emissions. When our society provided these companies with a near monopoly to produce the energy that powers our homes and businesses, we did not give them the right to poison our air and our water. GHG from burning fossil fuels is doing just that. You can change the rules governing utilities in ways that incent them to stop polluting our air and water. This is a fundamental human right.

The automobile, in all its forms, has given us enormous mobility. It is also responsible for 30% of greenhouse gases. If you require that the companies that manufacture cars and trucks be responsible for their emissions you will see an enormous shift away from fossil fuels.

It takes ¾ gallon of oil to produce a pound of beef. Raising livestock for human consumption, particularly cattle, is responsible for 50% of emissions worldwide due massive deforestation and its reliance upon fossil fuels. Switching to non-beef sources of protein would seem to be a no-brainer. How about one hamburger per month instead of one per day. While you're at it, choose sustainable materials for your home and your clothing. It may insignificant but everything adds up. Go to Climate Hero where you can calculate your own carbon footprint and find ways to reduce it.

Change is often slow, but it occurs. We regulated the chemicals that were damaging the Ozone layer and protected ourselves from the damaging rays of the Sun. We cleaned up toxic waste sites and stopped rivers from burning. Change is possible, but the old adage, "Action is louder than words" has never been more appropriate. Speak up but walk your talk.

Recycling, powering your homes and businesses with wind, water and solar energy, reducing the use of plastic and eating organically are all simple personal decisions that collectively can change the world. Do these things and you will become models for others.

And know that we are counting upon you. It is the young that go into battle, not the elderly, and we shall get behind you.

I challenge you and young people, from eight to eighty, to create a new and happier future. I shall continue to write and speak out, but the future belongs to you. Be bold with your ideas. Think big and ask for monumental changes. Challenge those in power with your ideas and your actions. When people say, "Why?" you say "Why not." Just as important will be the picture you paint of the more just, peaceful and livable world that we can create together. Show us the way and we shall follow.

All of your ideas may not float. Fortunately, you'll get some slack for being young and idealistic. As grandparents, we expect that from you. In fact, the world needs that from you. Now, more than ever.

When I tell you that "we know what to do," I am telling you that the world is full of people with bright and hopeful solutions. Whether you become a doctor, an engineer, a brick mason or a bartender seek out these people, study their habits, assemble them, develop plans and take action. Others will join you. From you I have discovered that most young folks are aware of the problem. They are looking for solutions. Be a solution.

Over the course of this book, I'm going to share stories of events that led to my earliest awareness of how our daily habits can create a planetary crisis and also of a dream I had that led me to a book that became my guide to implementing a low carbon lifestyle. For me it was the Integral Urban Handbook. I lived in a city, and it is still a good model, but I encourage you to discover your own. How am I doing? I buy organic produce, recycle, mulch my waste and drive an electric car that is fueled by sunshine falling upon my home's solar panels. I'm making progress, but there's much work to be done.

One last thing. On your journey about this remarkable planet we call Earth, your ethics will be tested. In this book I shall tell you about the good people that surrounded me when I was a child, the kind that showed up and measured up. They were the kind of people that gave me hope and the determination to overcome life's challenges. They were skilled, hard-working, thoughtful and dedicated to their families. For the most part they were selfless in ways that provided me with lessons, the kind of which, served as benchmarks against which I could measure myself and ask, "Am I good people?" We are sharing this planet with a kaleidoscope of people and creatures. Treat all creatures as you would want to be treated.

For me these good people, stretching over generations, have demonstrated the meaning, importance and value of a rare commodity I call integrity. They showed me that it is desired but often elusive. Highly valued but often neglected. And, although common to some degree in almost everyone, often subject to situational ethics. From these good people, my family, I discovered something simple about integrity. It is worth millions but costs only five cents . . . and it applies to everything in life.

May you be blessed with both the strength and the integrity to meet this and all your future challenges.

Contents

Interview with Ian Emerson Myers

Ian Myers is a junior at Oakwood High School in Oakwood, Ohio, a comfortable, tree lined suburb of Dayton, Ohio. Like many young people his age, he is juggling studies with a parttime job and athletic practices. His home is not currently threatened by rising seas, forest fires or floods. It was not always that way.

In the chapter entitled, "Let Your Dreams be Your Guide," I describe my effort to transform an 1840s structure into a modern, energy efficient home located in the Oregon Historic District of Dayton. On the walls of that home were water marks left by the Great Flood of 1913 which left much of Dayton under several feet of water. To thwart the repeat of this disaster the Miami Conservancy District constructed dams that created a series of reservoirs throughout the region. With the potential for flooding averted Ian believes, like many others, that he lives in a relatively safe place. Therefore, his observations about the dangers of global warming, the awareness of his classmates and the attention given to this threat by public schools provide insight as to the lack of urgency that this crisis demands.

GSM: In the book I talk about climate change. What is it and what is causing it?

Ian: Earth is changing faster than it should, and this is caused by people who use fossil fuels

GSM: In what ways is the earth changing too fast?

Ian: It is becoming too hot.

GSM: When did you first learn that our environment is being threatened?

Ian:	In elementary school we learned that the atmosphere is heating up due to the burning of fossil fuels and it is causing the ice sheets of Antarctica to melt.

GSM: Why is that a problem?

Ian: The melting ice is causing the oceans to flood communities all over the world.

GSM:	How big a threat is global warming to your generation?

Ian: I'm still learning about all of the consequences, but I am quite worried about its impact upon my future.

GSM:	In what ways do you think will it affect you?

Ian: It will impact where I choose to live in the future. Some places will be higher risks than others.

GSM:	You are studying math and engineering. What does it mean when scientists tell us we must reduce our carbon footprint? What do people or the government or the world need to do about it?

Ian: One's carbon footprint is the amount greenhouses gases that he or she creates by using fossil fuels like coal, gas and oil. To reduce one's carbon footprint we must use these fuels much more efficiently and find new ways, such as solar panels and wind energy, to get done what fossil fuels have been doing for us.

GSM:	Like powering our cars, homes and businesses?

Ian: Yes, we must switch to things like solar and wind energy.

GSM:	These are fields requiring engineering skills and you are studying engineering. Do you see yourself working with in any capacity on solutions to global warming?

Ian: Not at this time.

GSM:	I know it's early for you to be making career choices but would it help to know that climate solutions will become a huge industry over the next twenty years. There will be high paying jobs for many skilled people like yourself.

Ian: I know this is an important field but I have another career path in mind at this time.

GSM:	What can you do or are you planning to do to make things better?

Ian:	We all need to learn more about the problem and the solutions so that we can reduce our own carbon footprints. Right now, decisions about the car I drive and the way my home is heated are beyond my control but I am learning so that I'll be prepared when I'm on my own.

GSM:	That sounds like a message for everyone in your generation. How aware are your friends and classmates of the dangers caused by global warming?

Ian: They are aware that this is occurring, but they don't seem to care because it is not affecting them personally.

GSM:	Are you saying that the water has to be at their doorsteps to get their attention.

Ian: Probably.

GSM:	How does that make you feel?

Ian: Less than hopeful.

GSM:	Does your school provide any instruction or create any awareness of this topic?

Ian: No

GSM:	Should it?

Ian: I think schools should incorporate the challenge of global warming into existing classes such as chemistry and physics.

GSM:	What will it take for more people to understand this threat and take action?

Ian: It will have to impact them personally.

GSM:	The hurricanes, floods and fires are not enough to get their attention?

Ian: It has to be more obvious than a weather event. There have always been floods and hurricanes, so they are not connecting those events with their lives.

GSM:	What are the top three things you would you tell your generation that would help them connect to this threat?

Ian: First, become more aware. This is a big problem and it's not going away. Second, tell your parents about it and try to influence decision makers.

GSM:	Do you mean, write a letter to your congressman?

Ian: We can use social media to alert people. We can join clubs that have an environmental focus such as the Greenpeace, the

Audubon Society and the World Wildlife Federation. And we can get involved in events that attract the attention of the media.

GSM: What is number three?

Ian: Don't be held back by your age. If everyone does something it will help.

(Author's note: Greta Thunberg was 16 yrs. old when she appeared before the United Nations to chastise leaders for threatening the future of her generation by not acting to stop the burning of fossil fuels.)

GSM: What three things would you like everyone to know about the threat of global warming?

Ian: Number one, it's real. Two, do what you can. For instance, watch what you buy because every decision either adds to the problem or becomes part of the solution. Three, there is great power in groups, people acting together. Get involved with others and demand change. Change is possible.

GSM: One final question. I have painted a rather grim picture about the future for mankind. Are you still optimistic about the future?

Ian: Anything is possible. Many people are already trying to address this problem so there is hope.

Climate Fact:

Almost one gallon of oil is used to make a pound of beef which makes the cost of your hamburger as much about oil as it is about meat. Petroleum contributes 25% to the cost of a steak dinner. The space currently utilized for meat and dairy production takes up 1/3 of the habitable land on Earth.

What can you do about it?

Buy local foods, eat local foods and eat less beef.

Who are we?

"We can be what we think, but we are what we do."

"Stop!" I shouted. "There's a cop in the road."

That was the moment I discovered that my friend and former high school classmate, David Eaton, needed contact lenses. Why he left them at home I'll never know. Neither did I know how close to death we came that Friday evening in March until we skidded to a stop.

I managed only a sour glance at Dave. There wasn't time to remind him how easily the whole thing could have been avoided if he had heeded my suggestion a minute earlier. I was busy stuffing our illegal cargo under the passenger seat, but a case of beer and a couple bottles of Sherry take up more space than was available. In Michigan, being under twenty-one with that much booze in one's possession could get you a night in the hoosegow. We were only nineteen.

Due to his myopia, David hadn't seen the Michigan State Police Officer manning the roadblock. It was not Dave's first traffic incident involving alcohol. He had already survived two crashes, one of them the end over end variety.

As the officer approached our car another cop propped against his cruiser on the side of the highway and aimed a twelve-gauge shotgun at us. My pulse quickened with the severity of the situation. But these guys weren't looking for a couple of kids with fake IDs. They were armed for much bigger game. I was thankful they weren't the kind that shot first and asked questions later. They were obviously better trained than the juvenile delinquents that were given badges in our small town.

We soon found out that they were in search of two young men who had robbed a gas station in Kalamazoo, a few miles west of Delton and exactly where we were now parked in the middle of State Route 43. Three minutes ago, we had left a bar in this little burg with a twelve pack and some liquor David had acquired with a fake I.D.

What I couldn't store beneath the seat I tried to cover with my legs. Hoping that my body would conceal the goods I craned toward the driver's side window. The officer leaned into the window and pointed to the packages under my legs. When he asked, "What do you have in there?" I knew that the evening was not going to go as planned.

How did I get into such a mess? My folks were out for the evening and I was at my home in Hastings enjoying a weekend away from college. Dave and I wanted to wash down some snacks with a couple of beers while we watched the opening round of the NCAA basketball tournament. It was to be a tame affair. We drove about fifteen miles west of Hastings to a bar in Delton where Dave could use a dummied driver's license to buy beer. I found liquor to be toxic. Two beers made me silly, and a six-pack could provoke non-stop vomiting until three o'clock the following afternoon. I was dumfounded by the amount of liquor and beer Dave brought back to the car. It was more than I could tuck under the seat of our aging Oldsmobile. My first thought was to get it out of sight.

Caution is an attitude that I adopted early when around people who drink a lot. Every alcoholic I have ever befriended abused our relationship. They were people who drank obsessively. Their dependencies ultimately overcame the rudimentary requirements of friendship such as honesty and respect. It clouded sound judgment. My parents and some of their friends drank a lot when I was a child but they never combined it with driving cars. There were many weekends that included overnight stays by those fun-loving people. I must have learned how to engage in adult activities without causing harm to anyone. I have had my share of fun and good times but I never lost my wits nor my control due to alcohol and it wasn't going to happen that night, either.

David introduced me to beer and some of the guys on the athletic teams that were the biggest boozers. He was handsome and a competitive athlete. He possessed a mellifluous tongue and could quote entire passages from "Waiting for Godot," as if he was reading for a part in the play. He went on to earn a Masters Degree from BYU and do missionary work in southeast Asia. By that night, he was well on his way to becoming an alcoholic. I doubted that neither he nor I could elude our fates. We made a mistake. We got caught. We were going to have to take our medicine. I believe they cuffed us, but I don't recall for sure.

I was a rank amateur at what could be a dangerous activity for teenagers so I heeded the notion embedded by the time I was sixteen. There are things one does not do at that age in combination with alcohol. The entire incident could have been avoided if I had insisted upon what my common sense had dictated. I had spotted the cops when we pulled onto the highway after leaving the bar. They were too far away to see what we were doing so I instructed David to park in the driveway of a home across from the bar. He did that but then refused to get out of the car. He wouldn't open the trunk so that I could put the goods out of sight. From that distance, without his contact lens, he couldn't see well enough to make a wise decision. It was a simple oversight. He forgot to bring his glasses and it resulted in a weekend that most would prefer to avoid.

My father, I learned later, doubted that a weekend in a jail cell would create a lasting scar but believed it would serve as a major lesson. I can't argue with that. We create our own outcomes and must take complete responsibility. I should have insisted that Dave put the beer in the trunk or let me out of the car. I never held any ill-will toward David. He was my friend.

My grandfather, Fred Frey, wasn't concerned about the lesson that experience had to offer me. He was irate. Grandpa was not a man to drink. I never saw him with so much as a beer. And he was as honest as the day is long. He was one of the county's prominent farmers and a Grand Poopah and a lifetime member of the local Mason's order. He was well known by the Sheriff. He often flashed his big Masonic ring, especially after an officer had stopped him for even a minor infraction. In our small town that must have carried some weight because he was seldom bothered. Grandpa was not around when David and I were stuffed into the back of the patrol car. We would have to stay in the county lockup until a judge could convene court on Monday morning.

Neither my father nor my mother called or came to see me that weekend. I was surprised but too embarrassed to face either of them. When Grandpa got the news of our incarceration, I was told that he exploded. He assumed that the Sheriff should have realized that he had not captured another Al Capone, the famous mobster that ran illegal beer joints during Prohibition from 1920-1933. I was Fred Frey's grandson. Grandpa Frey felt that the Sheriff should have called him and then let me to go home until the matter was adjudicated. He was outraged that I had to spend one hour in jail and an entire weekend was preposterous! I was one of his eleven grandchildren so I had no idea how important I was to him at that time, but Grandpa knew that I wasn't an outlaw. I was just a kid who wanted to spend an evening with a friend and watch a basketball game. It was after my grandfather had passed away that I was reminded about his compassion and his effort to protect me during that challenging moment in my young life. I felt his embrace long after he was gone.

He provided me with one of life's enduring lessons. You help your family. The family is the foundation for the expression of love and everything else that matters. It all begins there. So it is with our family but we are a very independent bunch.

Memories of my family are fond and their impact has been lasting. They were simple people and probably like most Americans in their dreams and aspirations. They wanted to do important work, earn a decent living and spend time with their families. Their stories provided me with lessons that are timeless, the kind that helped guide me along my life's path.

We tend to develop a path for our lives that is a continuation of the combined paths of our parents. My father, George Louis Myers, was a practical man and a small-time entrepreneur. He was honest and spiritual and he was one of three children of a family of modest means that had to negotiate the Great Depression of the 1930s.

My mother, Joyce Elaine (Frey) Myers, was one of four kids who grew up on a dairy farm. She became an organizational wizard for an industrial truck manufacturer. She was smart enough to have never lost at Hearts (a challenging card game). And even though she was the youngest in her family, she was often called upon to keep her family intact. Those traits were apparent throughout her life. Therefore, the general path of my life resulted in the convergence of that spiritually centered, entrepreneurial soul with the consummate organizer whose family was the center of her life.

Most people don't really know themselves until they reach the age of fifty which can expose them to a certain degree of floundering for over half of their life. At your age, the road to fifty may seem a long journey. My revelation occurred during my fifties while on a trip to Amsterdam, and it wasn't too late. It resurrected accounts of our family that had become the stories of my life. The people who entreated me to study hard and seek the truth, led me to adventure, imparted wisdom, encouraged me, cajoled me, and at times threatened to wash my mouth with soap. They also provided me with the principles by which to live, made it okay for me to laugh at myself, and to reach deeper within myself when the going got tough. Those people became my heroes.

I am going to share their stories, and some of my own, with you. If these vignettes provide you with a model by which you can fashion your own life or help you avoid just one pitfall I'll be content. If they motivate you to pursue bigger dreams, have healthier relationships or make better decisions, I'll be further encouraged. If they entreat you to live each moment of your life with passion, encourage a thirst for knowledge and respect our home, planet Earth, and all the people on it, I'll be exhilarated!

To better understand and appreciate these stories, I think it is helpful to first answer this question: Who are we as a family?

My revelation regarding our family occurred in 1997 on a crispy late November afternoon after perusing the Rembrandt-Rijksmuseum collection of the master artists of the 17th Century Dutch Golden Era. I was hurrying to get to the Van Gogh Museum before closing. I was in Amsterdam to do research on a novel I was writing, a murder mystery with American pot prohibition set smack dab in the middle of it. Given Dutch leniency to public policy on that subject, Amsterdam seemed like the obvious place to collect a lot of data. To get further smack dab in the middle of it, I paid an entrance fee to a convention that carried with it the title of "Judge" in the 10th Annual Cannabis Cup that was being sponsored by High Times Magazine, the go-to rag for everything hemp. But that's another subject.

I took my judge job seriously, so time for museum hopping was limited, but I had carved an afternoon out of my schedule just for that purpose. Art would inform me of the culture and history of the Dutch people as much as my conversations in their coffee shops, the principal purveyors of legal weed. Within minutes of my arrival I found my face in every painting that decorated the walls of the Van Gogh Museum. Until that moment, one month after my fifty-second birthday, I had been under the impression that my ancestors were only English and German.

With the conference finished and the competition for the best weed completed (I chose Amsterdam Gold but it barely made it into the top five because the twenty-somethings that lit up before breakfast comprised a majority of votes), I headed back to U.S. soil.

There I put the question of heritage to my father and he said, "You didn't know that your grandfather was called Dutch Frey?" He was referring to Fred Frey, and I was dumbfounded! In fifty-two years no one had given me the slightest clue about that and it seemed like important stuff.

So, then I'm thinking, "Okay, I'm English and I'm Dutch, not German." That explained a lot and even though I do not believe in coincidences, one of my best friends in the world was named Stephen VanHecke. Van is as common to the Dutch as Smith is to Americans.

And there was another thing, too. Myers is an English name. Place an "e" after the "m" and it becomes a German name. Not mine. I didn't have that oddly placed "e" in my name. But my mother was Joyce Frey, not Fry. That is an extra letter with no apparent necessity unless you come from the homeland, The Netherlands.

There's more! I grew up a little over an hour's drive from a small, industrial west Michigan community called Holland. That's the same name most people call The Netherlands. This Holland sits along Lake Michigan. Each year in May everyone in town able to walk dons a pair of wooden shoes and marches down Main Street during the annual Tulip Festival. It doesn't get any more Dutch than that.

So, I was English and I was Dutch. And I was proud of it. The Dutch are very cool people. Their ability to combine fashion with function and economy makes them extraordinary. I saw it in their architecture, their furniture and their laws. Go into their bathrooms and look at the doorknobs, fixtures, and appliances. It was the same stuff that's in our bathrooms, but they're so much more economical in the use of space and resources. And they look so cool! They have a style that expresses economy but it is appealing to the eye and emanates an aura of sophistication. Right there I realized that those ideas were similar to my own.

In addition to Van Gogh and Rembrandt there were many Dutch painters and sculptures during the Golden Age whose work is still on display in museums throughout the world. During the last three months of 2006, the Dayton Museum of Art, in your hometown, had the works of Rembrandt and others on display. The Dutch practical side and industrious nature combined with their appreciation for the arts in ways that mimicked my own disposition. The way you feel when you put on new jeans that fit perfectly without any alteration, that's how it felt to learn that I had descended from Dutch genes.

Was I discarding my German heritage? No. There was some of that in me, and my rudimentary impression of Germany carried with it a reputation for prowess in engineering, an intellectually demanding discipline. Were it not for a sour experience with high school trigonometry I would have pursued an engineering curriculum. I've always liked high performance gadgets and knowing how things work, and the Germans gave me that in so many things from their cars to their beer. The German genes had brought some very positive qualities to my lineage. They had contributed to my industrious and disciplined nature. The problems I had with that attachment were the two wars (WWI & WWII) instigated by the Germans. They killed millions and millions of people and attempted the genocide of an entire culture, the Jewish people. Furthermore, I was raised by a man who had given two years of his young adult life to a military engaged in a war against Germany as well as Japan.

Like a good reporter, I felt the need for confirmation. During the annual family reunion, I shared my revelation with Norman Frey, a cousin on my mother's side of the family.

Norman said, "Grandpa Frey's nickname was Dutch, but it was spelled Deutsch."

What Norman said made sense. Deutsch is the language of Germany. My grandfather, Fred Frey, was German. I had to accept it. I am English and German. However, I knew that Germany and The Netherlands had shared a common border for centuries, and that their people and cultures had been mixing for most of that time. And I couldn't overlook the faces I saw in the Dutch art galleries that looked so much like my own. I am convinced that our family had evolved from the influences of the English, the German and the Dutch cultures.

It would have been nice to know about my heritage earlier in my life. It might have helped me understand my tendencies. It might have helped me understand why I chose various directions for my work and my life. It might have helped me understand the things that arouse real passion within me such as the music and the arts as well as the things that cause me great despair including prejudice, injustice and crass disregard for our environment. Maybe it would have helped me identify the traits of the woman with whom I would be the most compatible, my life's mate. With hindsight it was easy to see how knowing those things about my family would have been beneficial.

No one has recorded the family history. But my aunt, Donna Thompson, sketched out some aspects of our family tree. What I absorbed about our family came mostly from events and holidays spent with family members and a close connection with my grandparents.

For instance, when Grandma Grace (Myers) was approaching ninety she entertained me with tawdry stories of the townies I knew in my youth. That she had decided to share the kind of information that grownups had kept from me even as a teenager, the kind they tended not to share with their kids because it was mostly about sex, turned me giddy inside. It was also the kind of information that would have advanced my sexual maturity when it was desperately needed, in my teens and twenties. Here I was, way into my forties, and my grandmother made me feel as if I had finally gained membership in the adult club.

Those people, my own family, knew so much. Fortunately, I got to spend a lot of time with them, enough time with my aunts and uncles and cousins and grandparents that I couldn't help becoming affected by the strength of each one's character. They were honest in every way and blessed with the ability and inclination to love. The way in which they led their lives provided me with many of the lessons I would need to negotiate down the path of life.

As much as I learned about the rewards of hard work during summer jobs tending my grandparents' gardens or painting their house, I discovered an equal lesson in integrity in one afternoon at their produce stand.

Grandma Myers, a short but sturdy woman with gray hair and sensible black shoes, manned the produce stand in front of their home. From the leftovers of Grandpa's gardens, she made the most memorable lunches. They featured fresh chilled beef steak tomatoes, green and wax beans, and steaming sweet corn picked that very morning. The bread, home baked, came steaming from the oven. Add some real butter to that tasty cuisine and my need for red meat was overcome by the explosion of freshness in my mouth. My grandparents were not vegetarians but they were very healthy people who lived to the ages of 82 and 96. That proved to be of great importance when, in my late twenties, I decided to give up my carnivorous habits due to the undesirable health and environmental consequences of red meat consumption.

In those same gardens my grandfather, George Henry Myers, demonstrated that sustainable gardening, created with the limited use of pesticides and herbicides, produced better food while being environmentally friendly. That was to become an important aspect of my life and my health. If you want to live for a long time, choose your parents well. Otherwise, exercise and avoid red meat and the four white things: shortening (deep fried foods), refined white flour, sugar and salt.

One of the fondest memories of my other grandmother, Lola Frey, also involved food. I'll never forget the scrumptious pineapple cookies she baked that delighted my tummy and fogged the windows of her modest cottage as they came from the oven. The joy with which she served them was special. Her big eyes lit up as I stuffed them into my mouth one by one. With arms extended she was always there for me with the kind affection that every kid needs: cookies and love.

Grandmothers, food, and love came to me in the same package. Due to all that nurturing I am impelled to hug my own children every time I see them even though they are now in their forties.

Grandpa Frey was a tall and lanky man with an infectious smile and a soft but occasionally scratchy voice. He would shock us by removing his teeth (dentures) and placing them on the table next to a large ashtray meant for his cigar which was, as far as I knew, his only vice. He had been a successful dairy farmer for many years and, as the story goes, had once employed his own estranged father. My grandmother and he spent their summers at a cottage on a lake near their farm. To my delight I was a regular guest. During long hours in a twelve-foot aluminum boat powered by an aging six-horse Johnson motor, Grandpa showed me how to fish. He also explained how over-development and over-fishing can spoil a lake. It was a lesson I could apply to my home, to my country and even to my planet, and reinforced a developing theme in my life. Then I would sit next to him in his big car on the way to Halstead Market where he would buy me a "Safety Pop," a small cherry sucker on a soft rounded stick that couldn't impale my cheek if I fell on it. Grandpa was my teacher and my protector.

I was a sophomore in college the night the Barry County Sheriff detained me for underage possession of alcohol. Despite Grandpa's perturbations for this minor infraction, I was placed upon probation and told not to hang out with David Eaton. Had Grandpa been successful in keeping me out of jail I would not have minded going through life without that experience, but it turned out to be a wildly entertaining weekend.

The Barry County jail was spartan, replete with steel bars, wooden benches and concrete floors that left me with profound images. The first was seeing my cousin Larry Myers' name carved into the top of the wooden picnic table on which our meals were served. Larry had gone through a period of aberrant self-discovery while challenging parental authority in his late teens and found himself incarcerated as his reward. He survived, persisted and became a competent welder. I know Larry is an honest guy because he is a Myers. Later I'll tell you a story about Grandpa George (Myers) that helped me define honesty and its importance.

The other image from that weekend is the bullet hole through the heel of a weekend drunk who was dumped into the cell across from us. His claim to fame? He proclaimed to be a fast-draw artist and had faced James Arness, from early television's Gunsmoke. Each episode began with Marshal Dillon, played by Arness, in the midst of an old-west style gunfight on the main street of Dodge City. The Marshal won every time. To two such impressionable young fellows as us, this guy's story would have been credible, even impelling, if it weren't for the scars on his heel. That loser had been so incompetent he couldn't get the gun out of his holster before putting a cap into his own foot.

The jail contained three or four cells. Multiply that by the hundreds you find in big city lockups and you get an idea of how many bizarre characters the world has to offer. Had my grandfather been successful in interrupting my stint in the Barry County jail, I wouldn't have regretted it, but I would have missed a rare opportunity. Looking back, it was as if David and I were bystanders during the writing of a Carl Hiaasen novel, watching all of the weird characters pass through his imagination.

I went to Amsterdam to do research for a novel and came back with new knowledge of my heritage, a heightened awareness of the fascinating characters that have comprised our family, and an appreciation for the lessons they taught me. Let's start at the beginning.

Climate Fact:

One serving of apple sauce contains 37 different chemicals. Our food is filled with pesticide residues that both the U.S. and Canadian governments say are causing brain and liver damage, in addition to birth defects and lower IQs in children.

What can you do about it?

Eat organic fruits and vegetables. Pesticides don't taste very good!

Happiness is a choice

*"We're all in this together, but you can't allow others to
drag you into their muck."*

By the time I was five I had gotten a tattoo and run away from home. Times weren't tough, nor was I an unhappy child. To the contrary, tucked into the farms, forests, and lakes surrounding my small Michigan town while cradled within the arms of a loving family, I was enjoying my childhood. World War II had ended, and my parents, like most Americans, were back to the business of building a home, raising a family, having picnics and going to ballgames. My summers were spent camping, fishing, playing ball with my friends and running through the fields and barns of my uncles' farms. Life was good.

So, what inspired the tattoo and my desire to flee my home? Running away was my way of making a statement about which I'll tell you more later. The tattoo was a traumatic life-altering event!

Uncle Bob's farm (Robert Frey, your great grandmother's brother) was an unlikely setting for an ink shop, but that's precisely the place where the tattoo became permanently etched into my tender, three-year-old cheek. You can still see the faint outline of a quarter dollar-sized scar on the right side of my face just above the jaw line. It wasn't a back-alley ink-shop job where some burly, aging ex-Marine with a beer gut and an unruly beard initiated me after a drunken night on the town. I was only three, and it was put there by my uncle's dog.

That's right! I was attacked by a dog. But that tattoo is also there due to a combination of curiosity, some disregard for authority and stubbornness, a trait I had obtained the old-fashioned way. It was passed along to me.

The dog was no bigger than the average hound, but at three and a half I was no match for it. It wasn't as if I was trying to purloin something from the dog's bowl, nor was I provoking him. I was petting the little guy. Everyone petted that dog. I thought the dog liked it. Apparently not when it was eating!

I loved animals of all kinds, but I didn't get the chance to choose between a butterfly or a dragon or something that may have expressed my artistic urge or my willingness to accept animals as equals. There was no time to browse the photos on the wall of the tattoo shop to make a selection. It happened so fast. One moment I was an innocent child in the midst of a bucolic summer day on the farm, and the next I was on the ground, toppled by a normally playful puppy that I never imagined for an instant was not my friend. Up to then he had been like a teddy bear or a stuffed animal that I took to bed with me.

I was hurt but even more shocked! I had been told by Grandma Frey and her daughter-in-law, Mary (Uncle Bob's wife), not to bother the dog while it was dining. I didn't accept the wisdom of their words. It seemed so natural and innocent, an expression of affection, to pet the dog. How could the dog misinterpret such a gesture? It did, though, and the result was a gnarly gash on my cheek, an instant tattoo!

My grandmother kept the dog's bowl parked on the back step of her little cottage. It couldn't have been more than a hundred feet down the sidewalk from the main farmhouse where Uncle Bob and

Aunt Mary lived. My grandfather, Fred Frey, had worked that dairy farm on Route 37 between Hastings and Battle Creek, Michigan for many years before turning it over to his son, Robert. I was headed toward Grandma's house when the dog trotted by me. He got to the doorstep ahead of me and dipped his head into the bowl. In hindsight I supposed that was a matter of habit for him, checking for food whenever he passed that bowl, but that didn't occur to me. It wasn't dinner time yet and as far as I knew the dog ate dinner fifteen minutes after people did. That's when we dropped our table scraps into the dog's bowl.

As I reached the porch step I noticed something in the bowl, but I gave it little attention. I did what I had always done. I kneeled and laid my hand on the dog's back. It turned and, with a voracious growl, jumped onto me and etched a vaccine shaped impression into my left cheek. It became an instant reminder of my error each time I looked into the mirror for the next fifty years. "Let sleeping dogs lie and never bother them while they're eating." That is a piece of ancient wisdom I learned that day.

For me it was one of many lessons to be learned the hard way. I suppose that all people and all families have lessons to learn. My son, your Uncle Christopher Bradley Myers, borrowed a friend's bicycle when he was eight or nine and, without looking both ways, road into the path of an automobile. He was a trooper, barely squinting during the repair, but the sight of watching parts of his chin being stitched together was as painful to me as having my wisdom teeth pulled without an anesthetic. He incurred fender benders the first two times he drove a car by himself. Another time he ran his Jeep off the road during a snow storm. I laugh about it now because life offers lessons for each of us to learn. It's been said that we learn more from our mistakes than our successes. My encounter with the dog was surely a life altering lesson, but just the first of a series of events that have led me to the conclusion that the first goal of childhood is to survive it.

I hope that your learning experiences do not exact from you much in the way of limb or treasure, but there will be challenges that will serve as lessons for your life. Some may be minor such as falls from rollerblades or a line drive from a baseball. Some may be huge, of the teary eyed, gut wrenching type, and involve loss of a family member, a friend or a lover. I'm not projecting misfortune upon you. I'm just telling you that no one gets along unscathed. It is how you respond to these challenges that will set a pattern for your life.

I can't identify the source of my philosophy for handling these challenges, but having optimistic parents provided me with a solid foundation. My approach has been simple.

Whatever confronts you, stay positive. Take the high ground. It may not always be the easy thing to do when lurching out to assign or deflect blame seems appropriate, but it is necessary and it is more rewarding.

In spite of the fact that other people can cause us turmoil we are generally responsible for our own outcomes. Bad things do happen to good people, but we do indeed harvest what we sow. Accepting responsibility is part of integrity. Honesty fosters so many rewards and builds the character upon which we are judged. I guarantee that being positive requires less emotional capital and accelerates recovery from falls. It also makes us a hell of a lot more fun to be around than someone who thrashes around in the muck of despair and self-pity.

Nothing worthwhile comes without hard work and sacrifice. Relationship collapses, job losses, accidents, injuries, and the loss of family and friends will challenge you but you will carry on. You should. When faced with any challenge, happiness may become a chore but it is also a choice. It is a choice I made early in my life, and it is one that I practice every day.

Stay positive. Choose happiness.

Climate Fact:

The lights, phones, computers and appliances you leave on while not in use contribute to global warming and add 25% to your home's utility bill.

What can you do about it?

It doesn't get easier than this. Turn off idle lights, computers and appliances.

Stand your ground, but don't be stubborn

"Be discriminate, but do not be discriminatory. Be tolerant, but do not tolerate intolerance."

When I arose, it was going to be just another fun-filled, sunny summer day. What else was I to think? I was only four years old.

I had been warned about the train! If it came roaring toward me at a hundred miles per hour I could still see it for, at least, half a mile. But I was conflicted because mother had convinced me that as soon as I stepped with one foot between those rails I'd be squished.

Squished flatter than the bugs we stomped on the sidewalks with claw hammers. A friend and I crawled around the block on our hands and knees to smash the defenseless little critters. It was stupid and a giant waste of time when we could have been at the fish hatchery whopping bull frogs to lure to the big sturgeons.

We stunned the frogs with plastic whiffle-bats, tied strings around them and threw them into the pond in hope that those prehistoric fish would latch onto our makeshift tackle.

The sturgeon were legendary to us because we had heard about them but had never seen them. Reaching several feet in length they were one of the largest fish in Michigan and had been swimming in our lakes for millions of years. They had made an entire country, Russia, famous for its caviar.

One would occasionally grab the frog and run with it, but if we tried to increase the tension on the line, they would surrender both frog and line, probably because they grew tired of our game. Despite the near captures we had never spotted head nor tail of one with our eyes.

Anyway, the dilemma created by the train was not on my mind when I awakened that morning. Nor was any premonition that by day's end I'd be in the office of the county sheriff facing, Tiny Doster, the man with the badge.

It was 1949, and we lived on a tree lined street in a huge, two story house which house sat three blocks from the War Memorial Monument, a gigantic steel and stone statue that celebrated our country's victories in the World Wars.

A common site in many small towns, in our city the monument was situated smack dab in the middle of the intersection of Main and Broadway Streets. That was downtown Hastings, Michigan.

In another twelve years we were cruising the downtown strip in a 1950 Ford Coupe in the guise that we were cool enough to catch the attention of some local talent. I mean girls! There was little else to do after dark in a town with only one movie theater and a couple of drive-in restaurants.

It was a cheap thrill because the businesses that lined either side of Main Street took up only four blocks. We would drive from one end of Main Street to the monument, make a one-eighty around the big statue, and cruise back through the heart of Hastings. It wasn't South Beach or the Hollywood Boulevard, but it killed time on Friday nights when there wasn't a football or basketball game to attend. The real thrill came after high school golf practices. Six of us would cram into Barry Maguire's tiny Studebaker and race down Broadway. Mags could get the over-loaded automatic up to about fifty-five as we reached the hill that led across the Thornapple River on the way into the center of the city. At the very moment we began our descent he would kill the engine.

At first our goal was to make it around the big war monument. With thrusts and gyrations and a lot of cheering we were able to make a left turn around the monument and coast almost a block down Main Street. It was silly but it was harmless and it created lasting friendships. A few years later Mags and I would throw empty beer bottles against the fireplace in the basement of his fraternity house at the University of Michigan. The pile of glass on the floor was traditionally cleaned up at the end of each school year. At least, I think it was.

The train station was located between the top of the hill on Broadway and the War Memorial monument. The day of my big adventure must have been a Saturday because my mother was home that morning. During the week she worked at the Abstract Office in the County Building about three blocks from our house.

The County Building was next door to the jail and the office of the sheriff, Tiny Doster. Dad was away from home attending to one of his jobsites. After a short stint at Eaton Manufacturing in Battle Creek he became a masonry contractor and a damn good one. His sidewalks, porches, churches and fire-stations are still in use today.

After breakfast mother allowed me to play in the backyard while she did the laundry. Dad had hauled in a truckload of sand and dumped it between the back porch and the clothesline so that I could have a sandbox. After washing the clothes, Mother would run them through the wringers of the washing machine on the porch and then hang them upon the clothesline. After they dried, if I buried my face between their fluffy layers, I could still smell the sun and the wind in them.

It was a small yard for such a large house, and we shared that clothesline with the other renters. The Pugh family lived in the apartment on the other side of the house and a kind, old man named Shorty Devereaux lived above us. I would run into Shorty as he climbed the steps to his apartment on the second floor that we shared with him or in the hallway to the second-floor bathroom, also a shared arrangement. By the time we moved to our new home across town, midway through my fourth grade, I was almost as tall as him and I finally understood how he got the name Shorty.

But anyway, by mid-morning I was restless because it was Matinee Saturday at the Strand Theater. The Strand was the only movie house in town and only four blocks from my front door. I could ride my imaginary horse through the neighbors' backyards and alleys on my way home from all the Gene Autry, Roy Rogers and singing cowboy movies that the Strand could squeeze into an afternoon. We were stunned when The Strand raised the price of admission from twelve cents to twenty-five cents. We had a tough time coming up with a penny or two. How were we going to muster another thirteen cents? I knew immediately that price jump was destined to change my Saturdays.

That day I wanted to know if my neighbor, Tommy, who was only a year younger than me, wanted to accompany me at the movies. I ran between the sheets with my hands in the air to feel the warming cotton on my skin. It was like swimming in the clouds. I drifted away from the backyard and before long I was a half block from home and in front of Tommy's house.

In hindsight, as a parent I can understand my mother's reaction when she found that her son had vanished between loads of white and colored clothes. She panicked and her reaction was prompt.

She found me half way to Green Street, one of the busiest routes in town, and looped a piece of rope around my waste. When she returned with me to finish her chores she tied the other end to the clothesline. In addition to socks, underwear and work clothes I was tethered to the clothesline in my back yard.

I was sure she had violated my Constitutional right against cruel and unusual punishment. But that's another issue.

My mother was a warm and loving soul who offered guidance without the need of a stiff paddle. She made me feel as if I was the center of her attention. She held my hand as we walked the midway of the carnival at the Barry County Fairgrounds three blocks from our house, and she carried me in the basket on her handlebars when she went for a bicycle ride with Dad.

She also had a quick wit and a wonderful sense of humor, and she could take decisive action, when necessary, to remedy a problem. That day, I was the problem, and she was not going to take any more time to search for her wandering boy. Hence, I was restrained. At the time, despite of my love for her, I considered her response an exaggerated, flat out abuse of parental power.

I now know that being a Myers comes with a predisposition toward the pursuit of independence and freedom. You may suggest a behavior to us but we don't respond favorably to commands. Provide us with the facts or, at least, a modicum of supporting information if you want our allegiance or participation on most matters. This comes as natural to us as the tide does to the ocean.

Being tied to a clothesline in my own backyard was not only a violation of what I considered my genetic code, it was humiliating. It took me only minutes to devise an escape. As soon as mother was out of sight I freed myself from the rope and slipped into the garage. I grabbed my tricycle and headed out with only the clothes on my back.

It was difficult to get up any speed on a tyke's trike, but as I made the turn onto Broadway, a block from home, I thought I was in the clear. I glanced over my shoulder and Mother was not behind me.

I wasn't equipped for an overnight stay, having left home wearing only shorts and a short-sleeved shirt, but it was my first attempt at leaving home. It resulted, I suppose, from the kind of reaction that occurs when the doctor taps your knee with his little rubber mallet.

Nevertheless, I shifted into overdrive and cruised past the intersection that led to the A&P, the largest grocery store in town. I was headed for Tyden Park. It was a straight shot, only four blocks ahead of me, and downhill as soon as I passed the War Memorial Monument.

It hadn't occurred to me that someone might take an interest in a four-year-old on a tricycle crossing busy downtown streets all by himself. Soon I was to discover that someone had ratted me out. Mother later told me that one of her girlfriends had seen me peddling solo down Broadway and called to alert her. If I were inclined to hold onto a grudge that would have been the time for it, but there were more consequential obstacles ahead of me as I peddled onward.

At the monument I waited for the traffic to clear, and looked both ways before crossing. Once on the other side of Main Street I could see my first dilemma approaching. Halfway between the monument and Tyden Park, where there were swings, slides, and a playground full of fun awaiting, was the train station and, of course, the threat I had not considered when I fled from my overbearing mother.

No one was following me as I came to a stop at the railroad tracks. Freedom, only six feet away, was on the other side of those cold steel rails. I looked long and hard in each direction. I neither saw nor heard anything. There was no train. Even so I was absolutely paralyzed, filled with trepidation. I sat on my little tricycle as if I had been bronzed in time. I was angry at mother for tying me up and determined to make a statement. I was standing my ground but unable to go forward.

Mother's admonition gripped me tighter than any rope around my waste, and it overpowered all my will: "Do not cross those railroad tracks alone!"

I waited and waited until a familiar voice broke the silence.

"Spencer, Spencer! Stay right there!" she said. Mother approached on a dead run.

Although I knew she had come to take me home it wasn't an angry voice, and I wasn't disappointed that she had intercepted me. She had saved me from my dilemma and quelled my greatest fear. I may not have made it to the park, but I wouldn't have to cross the tracks alone. When she got close I saw both fear and relief in her eyes. She turned me around, gave me a little push up the hill, and I peddled for home.

I had made my statement and was feeling somewhat smug until we crossed Broadway Street at the monument. Her office was on that street but it was closed on Saturday. Why had we crossed the street? She didn't say a word until we reached the Sheriff Department at the end of the block. Now what?

"Leave your bike outside," were her only words.

My hand was locked within hers as she led me up the steps into the Sheriff's office. Inside were desks and chairs but no kids. There were only adults, some of whom wore uniforms. They apparently knew my mother because she pranced me straight into Sheriff Tiny Doster's office without any interference.

I was only four but I understood the purpose of the police. My Mom must have decided that I was too young to comprehend the "Fear of God" so she opted to intimidate me with the full weight of the law. I was dismayed, but I wasn't afraid. I hadn't done anything wrong.

The sheriff sat me in a large wooden swivel chair so big that my feet couldn't touch the floor. He stayed behind his desk looking very official. Mother explained what had happened and then sat quietly as the Sheriff ran through a litany of clichés about the dangers of running away from home. Their intentions were noble, but I couldn't get past the issue of credibility. Why had neither of them noticed the proverbial elephant in the room, the Sheriff. He was an aging, rotund man of no less than three-hundred pounds. He was grossly overweight, and I couldn't understand how such a man could be called Tiny. So, struck by that incongruity, I overlooked the fact that Mother had left out the part about tying me to the clothesline. That had to be illegal.

The ordeal ended without anyone being locked up. I rode home safely. Mother finished her chores while she waited to share the news of her runaway child with my father. I missed the matinee that day, but there were no lectures, no threats, no spanking, and I was never again tied to a clothesline.

I don't know if there is a moral to this story, but standing one's ground in defense of principles such as liberty, fairness and justice or coming to the aide of those whom are weaker or less privileged seems appropriate and admirable. It's part of our heritage and it certainly seems to be in the Myers' genes.

Adhering to behavior or a point of view in the face of impelling evidence to the contrary or in a way that demeans or disenfranchises others, is just plain stubbornness and it's neither fair nor just. I admit to possessing a bit of each of these traits. I can only hope that any of the genetic qualities that may have been passed to you have been done so in balance and that you never feel compelled to run away from home.

Climate Fact:

Forests soak up more global warming gases than all of the oceans combined. Each year we cut down enough forests to cover twenty million football fields.

What can you do about it?

Plant a tree. Grow a garden. Plant a tree. Grow a garden. Plant a tree . . .

Integrity is worth a fortune, but costs only five cents

"If you find something that is not yours, return it."

"Dad!" I screamed as a monster from the Black Lagoon took me into the depths of Wall Lake. "It's huge!" I said.

My bobber was nowhere in sight so I snapped back and pulled up on my cane pole. Something humongous had taken my hook, line and sinker to the bottom. I shifted to the right and then to the left in attempts to gain an advantage. The pole bent but the line gained no slack. Dad seemed ready to help even as he held his own gear steady.

Fishing from a row boat is mostly about silence and patience, commodities not common to a nine-year-old. Even so I had been sitting quietly and concentrating upon the tiny red and white cork bobber as it danced upon the waves. I had been taught to look for any unusual movement. A tilt or a slight downward movement suggested a fish was biting.

Fortunately, I had learned to differentiate between a real bite and the subtle rocking caused by the waves. What I felt was anything but subtle. I had been fishing with my father and my grandfathers for years but had never felt this kind of weight on my line. Since I had never caught nor seen a really big fish being caught I had to consider the possibility that the Creature from the Black Lagoon, as in the movie, was only a few feet beneath our boat.

Wall Lake was one of the thousands of small lakes that had made Michigan famous as a paradise for hunters and fishermen. Living within it were prized Walleye Pike and Pickerel that could reach two feet in length and weigh 10-20 pounds or more. I was used to catching fish not much larger than my father's hand, an occasional bass or bullhead, and a mudpuppy on one occasion. They're called Mudpuppies because they have four legs, are smaller than tiny Bassett hounds and have bodies that seem as if they're made of rubber. None of those put this kind of strain on my line. What if it's a pike or a really big largemouth bass? Those guys weigh a lot, too. Wow! This was going to be my best summer vacation ever. That is if I could get the giant thing into the boat.

I had been getting into and out of row boats since I was old enough to swim which was made possible because my father threw me off the dock one day. "Swim," he'd said. Thus, I had enough fishing experience to accept the possibility of another option. The fish had taken me into the weeds or gotten me stuck under a log at the bottom of the lake. Those large fish got big because they were smart. I had to be careful. My lightweight tackle was intended for pan fish such as perch, sunfish and bluegills. If I was too forceful, I might break the line. I couldn't let that happen.

In addition to the joy that would ensue from snaring the "big one," there was major status at stake. I was eager to become part of the lore that this family of fishermen had created over the years. Few things are as hollow and disheartening as having to say, "The big one got away." I tried everything my mentors had taught me until my exhilaration edged toward despair. That sinking feeling in the pit of my stomach insinuated that the "big one" might get away. I was rocking between two extremes of emotion at the same time.

Let me put that summer trip into perspective. I always looked forward to those two weeks each summer. Wall Lake was surrounded by fulltime residences, but we rented a cottage. My brother was not yet born so my sister and I each had separate rooms as we did at home. Mother would take a vacation from her job as Executive Secretary to the Vice President of Marketing for Clark Equipment Company, and Dad would drive back and forth from construction sites to the cottage. Summer was Dad's busiest season so he couldn't take the time off. I spent my days swimming, playing ball, and waiting for Dad to return so that we could go fishing.

Fishing had become an integral part of the family legacy. My father looked forward to two times each year. The first was when the ice formed on the lakes in Michigan so that he could chop a hole in it and fish through it. The second was when the ice thawed on the lakes in southern Canada. He would tramp through the wilderness with his friends carrying a pack on his back and a canoe over his head. They would spend a week fishing for trout. There is nothing more delicious than fresh trout, and I suppose they're even better if you've caught them yourself. Dad wasn't just a skilled fisherman. He was a rugged outdoorsman. He knew how to take care of himself in the "bush" as he called it. He had survivor skills. That was a place one would confront more bears and moose than people. At his campsite he once constructed an oven from aluminum foil and baked fresh bread for the whole group. Later he built an entire log cabin in the woods.

My father inherited his lust for the outdoors. It was almost impossible to name a lake in the lower peninsula of Michigan that George Henry Myers, my grandfather, he had not fished. I had seen him walk onto the ice and chop a hole amid a dozen other folks, all waiting for some sign that there were even fish living in the lake. He would catch his limit before his feet got chilled and walk off while the others scratched their fur hats in disbelief.

The Myers men were accomplished anglers. I was not. Years later my brother, Timothy Marc Myers, would accompany our father on his excursions into the bush. My grandfather, father, my uncle and my brother were accomplished at fly fishing, something that requires dexterity and technique. My proclivity had not evolved as had theirs. Frankly, I didn't want to give up the time I might spend looking for a girlfriend while eluding bears or fending off flesh-devouring black flies in the Canadian wilderness. I enjoyed camping but I've always preferred indoor to outdoor toilets and the soothing effect of a hot shower. I was, however, affected by their expertise, and I really wanted to have my own fish story.

Until that day I had only one story to tell and it was by way of a third party. My Grandpa Myers had earned a serious reputation in the fishing world as an aficionado. A friend of my mother named Richard, who was a photographer and an avid fisherman, confirmed my grandfather's fame with this account:

"I found out about a lake, not far from Hastings, that was supposed to be one of the best fishing holes in the area. I didn't know what it was called or how to find it because it was private. One day I finagled my way into an invitation. The next Saturday morning I packed fishing gear into my car and drove to the lake, about 30 minutes from Hastings, on snow covered country roads. I lugged my gear up and over a long hill that overlooked a small lake. In normal weather conditions I would have been able to see across the lake, but in a steady predawn snowfall I could barely make out the lone figure sitting atop a five-gallon bucket. The stranger stayed focused upon the line he had dropped through a rapidly freezing film of water in a jagged twelve-inch hole. I walked straight toward him. When I was only a few feet away your grandfather looked up, smiled and said: Good morning, Dick."

We went fishing like golfers play golf, always searching for a new and rewarding venue. Several times each year Dad would awaken me at two a.m. to begin our trek to Lake Michigan to fish off the piers at Holland or Grand Haven. We would pick up Grandpa Myers, stop for breakfast along the way and time our arrival to be at the boat launch that would take us to the piers at daybreak. At the Big Lake, as Lake Michigan was known to the locals, Grandpa would string two hooks onto his line and proceed to catch two eight to ten-inch perch at the same time. A crowd would often gather to watch him at work. It's called fishing, not catching, because it is not easy. Most people had trouble catching one and he was catching two at once.

I learned a lot about fishing from my grandfather, much about gardening, and even more about life. When I was in high school, my grandparents managed a produce stand in front of their home at the corner of Grand and Benson streets in Hastings. It was supplied by the many vegetable gardens Grandpa cultivated around town. Grandpa was a talker, actually a debater, about almost anything if he knew something about the subject.

One early afternoon, during one of his lengthy conversations with a customer, he forgot to give back her change for the sweet corn she had purchased. Later that day, after toiling in his gardens, he recalled his mistake, got into his 1953 Chevy, and drove across town to return a nickel to the woman.

One summer Grandpa returned from his gardens and laid down for his normal afternoon nap. It normally followed one of Grandmother's succulent lunches of sweet corn, wax beans and baked bread. He never woke up. I am sure he left this world, not only with a full stomach, but content that he had lived an interesting life and he had done it on his terms. He had persevered challenging times without compromising his integrity.

It is also easy to expect that everyone who attended his funeral, one of the largest the city of Hastings had ever known, had his own version of the "five-cents" story. You will never get everyone to like you, but George H. Myers, my grandfather, had earned the respect and trust of most people by the little things he had done for them for eighty-two years. He taught me about fishing, gardening and a lot more.

Fishing with these men had educated me about the delicate balance of man with nature. My other grandparents, Fred and Lola Frey, had a home on a lake, and I often heard Grandpa tell my father how over development on the lake had led to over fishing and a degradation of the water supply. Too many poorly designed septic systems had polluted the water and that isn't healthy for the fish or fowl.

Too many nutrients in the water choke the oxygen supply and lead to an abundance of algae and other vegetation that limits the number and size of fish. Over-fishing upsets the balance of wildlife. Eliminate the small fish and the large fish have no food supply. Take out too many larger fish and only the small fish survive, but their size is threatened because their predators are reduced so they can over-breed. It became clear to me that the actions of people could despoil a lake, a river, an ocean and upset the balance on our planet. The place where we live. In this infinite universe, I call it home.

Growing up with Depression Era elders also meant that we were cautious about the use of everything. We bought new things only when the old ones were thoroughly worn out. We re-purposed every item we could. Old five-gallon paint buckets could be cleaned out and refilled or sold in bulk to large manufacturers from out of town. Anything made of metal that broke was sold as scrap metal. Worn bicycle inner tubes would be cut up and wrapped around our bicycle hubs to prevent the buildup of grease. Punctured inner tubes from the car would be patched and used as rafts at the local lakes or swimming holes. We put screws into broken bats and taped the handles if they broke before the baseball season ended.

A summer garden was a necessity for fresh vegetables. "Waste not, want not" was not only the operating mantra in our home, it was almost a religion. To this day, whenever I leave a room there is still a voice in the back of my mind instructing me to, "Turn out the lights!" With global warming and climate change such a serious threat, this is as useful advice today as it ever was. It forever imprinted the concept of conservation on me.

As I struggled with what was on the other end of my line I recalled a trick that Dad had taught me. I created as much slack in the line as possible in hope that whatever had usurped my hook might interpret the slack as a form of capitulation and make a break for open water. I was wrong.

Until then Dad had played the observant and supportive role, but I was happy he decided to apply the veteran's touch. We had no sooner traded fishing poles than with one quick maneuver he freed the line, and it started rising to the surface. I shook my head. How did he do that?

"Uh oh." It occurred to me that it may have been too easy. My hopes dropped as suddenly as the tackle that had most certainly been snapped from the line. I was sure we had lost it.

I still have no idea whether it was Dad's uncanny technique or that the fish had tired of my battle with him, but moments later Dad lifted the monster into the boat. When it hit my hook, I knew I had latched onto something special. I wish I had been able to get that prize into the boat entirely on my own, but I was thrilled he had saved it. It was a thirteen-inch perch. Dad said it was the largest one he had ever seen. This time the "big one" didn't get away, and I had my own fish story to tell.

Climate Fact:

The trucks and cars we drive are responsible for 20% of greenhouse gases.

What can you do about it?

Drive an electric vehicle and fuel it with the sunshine that falls on your roof every day . . . and make driving fun again.

If you are entrusted with any responsibility prove you are worthy

"The universal laws of nature provide us with enough evidence that we are part of something enormous and not the center of it."

"Bang! Bang!" The report of a double-barreled shotgun broke the silence and almost knocked me off my seat.

Deep in the thickness of a west Michigan hardwood forest on a cool October afternoon those shots penetrated the silence like a street corner collision. I jumped to my feet.

I'd been scouring the treetops for half an hour looking for a squirrel or anything that would allow me to fire my new single barrel twenty-gage shotgun. That those woods were full of squirrels, rabbits, and partridges I was certain, or Dad wouldn't have driven us thirty miles to that specific location. Other than the sound of a few leaves scratching the branches as they drifted to the ground, I hadn't seen or heard as much as a cawing crow.

Down the valley on the opposite ridge I heard a rustling. I'd been perched under a tree, adhering to Dad's version of the old Chinese proverb: "Sit by this river and over time everything will pass by you." He seemed confident that I could distinguish between a red squirrel and the brown and burnt orange hues of the Fall canopy while trying to keep my hands warm against the cold steel of my gun.

It seemed an eternity since he had meandered down the valley with that powerful double barrel twelve-gage cradled across his arms. Until that shot I hadn't moved an inch for fear I'd frighten a squirrel or miss the movement of some target a hundred yards away.

In the serenity of the woods, the sound of leaves and twigs cracking under foot announced that something was moving my way. Then the sound turned into running. I had no idea how much anxiety could be provoked by the sounds of gunshots and running! It wasn't my first hunting excursion with Dad, but my ten-year-old heart crackled like cold rain bouncing off hot rocks.

No one was visible yet, but it had to be Dad, and he must be chasing something. Uh oh! If I couldn't see him in his camouflaged hunting gear, maybe he couldn't see me donned in patterns that easily blended into the Autumn landscape. I stood as stiff as a cutting board behind the tree, almost afraid to peak, for fear another shot would send stray buckshot in my direction.

I grew up in a family of hunters and learned gun safety including how to carry a gun in company and how to park my gun before crossing a fence. I had been taught this early and, of course, I learned not to point the weapon at others and never to run it. By age ten I had practiced at a local shooting range and had been hunting with Dad many times. I was comfortable around shotguns, the principle weapon used for small game and deer hunters in Michigan, but I considered them to be very dangerous.

I was shocked on October 16, 1955, four days before the opening of small game season, when Dad gave me a single barrel twenty-gauge shotgun for my tenth birthday. I was thrilled to have my own gun and enthralled by the trust that Dad had placed in me, but I knew this was accompanied by an awesome responsibility. It was more than a gun. It was a symbol of passage from boyhood to manhood, akin to a bar mitzvah for me, and from that moment I would have to do everything I could to retain his trust.

"Crunch. Crunch. Crunch!"

Dad came toward me at a sprinter's clip. He was dodging tall oaks, leaping over small bushes and he was running with a gun.

I looked for game down the valley in the direction he was running, but I saw nothing. He didn't break stride as he passed and pointed toward the treetops ahead of me.

"Stay on that side," he shouted.

I didn't know what he was chasing, and I was leery of following him. It wasn't just a matter of safety. Dad had been a football and track star in high school and I knew that I couldn't keep up with him while toting a gun almost my height and half my weight. He disappeared from view soon after passing me.

"Bang!" Another shot echoed through the valley. That one made me jealous. My gun was deafeningly loud and pounded my shoulder with its retort, but the point of having a gun is to shoot it. I wanted to shoot my gun but it was dangerous to fire aimlessly in the woods. That's how people got killed. As a result of that universal urge I've always wondered why guns are allowed in urban areas. Within minutes Dad returned. His pace had slowed and his gun was resting in the nook of one arm.

"What was it?" I asked and expected him to tell me he had seen a deer. I was aware of Dad's approach to deer hunting. He would shoot a buck almost anytime and get the license to hunt it later. Except on your own property it was illegal to shoot a deer without a license granted specifically for that purpose.

"Fox squirrels, two of them," he said in a business-like fashion.

Fox squirrels were rather large, reddish brown, fury rodents that were a staple of small game hunters in western Michigan. After mother flowered and pan fried them they were quite tasty. Rabbits were much sweeter and less gamey in flavor, but more difficult to hunt. Either were targets when Dad and I went for a hunt.

If the commotion hadn't sent most of the animals in the woods to the exits, they had certainly gone into hiding. The calm was noticeable. With dusk not far off, Dad set us on a course that would lead back to his truck, a pickup to which he had added a series of metal bins and drawers to house the tools of his trade.

Other than a brief stint in an Eaton Manufacturing water sprinkler plant in Battle Creek after his release from the Navy, he had been a masonry contractor. He learned electrical work from his brother, Tom Myers, and plumbing from others in the trades. He could also weld and operate all kinds of tractors and heavy construction equipment.

Every boy wanted to drive a truck or a tractor, including me, and that Dad did it, as if he had been born sitting upon one, was really impressive. With help from his friends, we had constructed our first home from the ground up. He never did anything "half-assed" as he referred to the cheap competition, and his work stood the test of time.

There are restaurants, churches, fire stations and residential additions all over western Michigan still standing that he constructed over fifty years ago. He paid his employees more than a fair wage and could be seen at most job sites up on the scaffolds laying blocks with his crew, another sign of the physical prowess in which he took great pride.

I was aware of my father's feats in sports by the accounts of his playing days in high school and his recruitment by the Western Michigan University, but that burst through the woods demonstrated a level of athleticism that made those stories come to life. Dad never boasted when he told his stories. It was his way of sharing some lesson he had learned along the way. He was five-foot-eight and two hundred pounds, about forty pounds over his weight in high school, but on this day I learned that he was as good as the stories I had heard. When arthritis severely limited his strength and endurance at age forty-eight, he told me it was the greatest challenge to his self-esteem he had ever experienced.

Thus far my father had seen a couple of squirrels, gotten off a few shots and had a good run. I had zip, nada, bupkis to show for the afternoon and was beginning to question my prowess as a hunter. Nevertheless, I stayed alert and scanned the trees overhead for anything that moved.

We were within view of our ride home when I heard something overhead. A medium-sized fox squirrel had jumped from one branch to another of a tall maple tree we had just passed. I turned around, pointed my gun upward and waited for the little critter to settle on a limb. Old growth maple trees can reach five to seven stories high, easy range for Dad's twelve-gage. An old twenty-gage with a misaligned barrel in the unsteady hands of a ten-year-old provided the target with, at least, even odds at that distance. Dad said nothing while I took aim. I just hoped the squirrel wouldn't move to the back side of the tree or jump to another before I had lined up a clean shot.

"Bang!" The recoil slammed the stock against my shoulder and the sound almost deafened me. I never got used to that. In spite of the bent barrel and my poor aim the squirrel was knocked off its feet. A rush of pride engulfed me. I hit it! I actually hit it! The feeling was momentary. Several limbs broke the animal's fall and upon landing, it scurried toward the hollowed trunk of an old oak that was rotting on the forest floor. Dad rushed to block the entrance, but he was late. I had wounded the little critter and created a new dilemma.

We could hear the wounded squirrel but it was beyond our reach. The light from above was dimming. Oh no! Darkness was going to complicate things even more. I looked at Dad with a "now what" face.

"We need a saw," he said with no emotion.

His truck didn't carry the kind of saw we needed for this job, so we would have to drive all the way home and back in order to remove the squirrel from the tree. I was already tired and deflated by the time we returned to the woods. Then I heard the sounds of suffering in that decaying log tomb. My poor aim had taken most of the fun out of this hunting adventure.

It was pitch black when we finished the job, and neither of us spoke more than a couple of words on the way home. Even so, it had become a memorable day. It was impressed upon me what a remarkable athlete my father had been. I was honored by the trust he had placed in me on my tenth birthday. And I learned that hunting was not a sport for my father.

"You eat what you kill and you never leave a wounded animal to die. It's cruel," he'd said.

Those were concepts that would guide me through any forest or any city for years to come

Climate Fact:

What you wear makes a difference. The fashion industry is responsible for 10% of GHG (Greenhouse Gas), 20% of water pollution and 10% of plastic waste. The average fashion garment is worn seven times before it is discarded. Less than 10% of clothing is recycled.

What can you do about it?

You got to look good, but you don't need all that polyester. Choose natural fibers. They feel better, last longer and they're not-made from oil. Re-use and recycle. Go retro.

Pride

"Let go of me!" Ronnie shouted as he struggled in vain to free himself.

My legs were wrapped around his torso and I had his head in an arm-lock. I wasn't trying to hurt him, just immobilize him, but there was no escaping my vice-like grip. Ronnie was a tough, brawny kid, a year older and bigger than me, and he had been a pain in my ass since our family moved into the neighborhood midway through my fourth grade.

I never bothered him so his annoying antics came as a surprise to me. I knew nothing of alpha male behavior.

Ronnie's attacks began as verbal barbs. Then came the name-calling. Kids hate being labeled as sissies, chickens and the sort of things meant to demean them. So did I.

The attacks normally occurred to and from our walks to elementary school and continued into Junior High School. He escalated the verbal attacks by knocking off my hat and running off with it. Other times he took my book bag or anything else he could grab. The legal term for that behavior is robbery.

Ronnie really wanted me to start a fight with him. Then he could claim he had grounds to beat me into submission. That would solidify his superiority in the neighborhood, a kind of alpha male behavior common in the animal world. The other kids on the block were not his match and never intervened. I guess he felt that I was the main obstacle to his being the King of the Apes in our neighborhood. I can't say I didn't fear Ronnie, and over time my tolerance of his aggressions may have led some of my friends to the erroneous assumption that I was easy prey. Some of them tried to follow in his footsteps. Ronnie was a bully.

My father had always encouraged me to think with my head as opposed to my knuckles. I didn't like to fight. That was a good thing because I was slightly built, not threatening in size or attitude, and it was one of the reasons my grip on Ronnie was mostly an attempt to get his attention. It wasn't the primary reason, though, I didn't pummel him into a bloody pulp, punishment I knew, even at the tender age of eleven, that I was capable of inflicting.

I suppose I tolerated his abuse long after most kids would have gotten a bloody lip defending themselves. I feared something else much more than Ronnie. I feared he would one day drive me to the edge and regret it. I was afraid of my own temper. I knew I would hurt him. I would hurt him badly, and I feared leaving him with the kind of scars that are slow to heal. Scars that would endure beyond childhood. That was not something I wanted to carry with me for the rest of my life.

Why was I so confident about the pain I would cause him? I wasn't a big kid but anger and intense resolve are powerful drivers. I am talking about the kind of anger and resolve that elevates a strength beyond what Ronnie Miller could imagine. I would hit first and I would hit hard. Bruises, welts, black eyes, torn clothes and tears would follow. They wouldn't be mine. He couldn't imagine that because he was a bully, driven by insecurity and low self-esteem.

Bullies come in all sizes, shapes and colors but have one thing in common. They are weak-willed beings, often with overbearing parents, and they are soft in the middle. A solid punch to the gut or one directly on the nose seems to get their attention like nothing else.

I was a happy child, having grown up within the cocoon of a loving family. Getting into a fist fight was contrary to my nature. I resisted the temptation to allow confrontations with bullies or wannabes to result in that outcome. I persevered as long as I could.

Eventually I realized that a punch or two in the right place was the medicine those misfits needed to set them straight. Ronnie turned out to be the catalyst for my education on this subject. When someone harassed me until I could no longer endure it, the confrontation with Ronnie demonstrated to me that it took only a couple of well-placed jabs to reset the kid's attitude.

In spite of that revelation I hated losing my temper, and I hated losing my friends. After four or five of those encounters those kids, former playmates, seldom came around again. Of course, they never bothered me again, but it didn't make sense that I had to beat up my friends to get them to treat me with respect. I came to accept that people who treated me with such little respect were not friends at all. I found out that kids can be very mean and that growing up is complicated.

The aftermath of those skirmishes was always the same. My father would get a telephone call from an irate parent.

"My kid came home crying today! He said your son beat him up."

Dad listened without interruption.

"Spencer knocked him down and jumped on top of him. He wouldn't let him up and his clothes are all muddy!"

It was always the same refrain.

"What are you going to do about this?"

My father's response was always the same. "I guess you should keep your son away from Spencer. Apparently, he doesn't like being bullied!"

Nothing more was said. Dad knew that I didn't instigate the fights, and he seemed to know who were the bullies.

He never once said to me, "Good job!" or "Way to go!" In fact, he never encouraged me to fight anyone. He was more inclined to say, "Study hard" or "Play hard or "Play fair."

He did encourage me to suppress my emotions or, at least, to focus them. Maybe that's why, once they surfaced in anger, I was so capable of overwhelming the protagonists in my life. With hindsight I can say that it is probably better to control emotions than to suppress them.

Anger can cause some serious damage, the kind I did not want to inflict upon others. In spite of the fact that my father never encouraged me to fight with anyone, he never objected when I tamed the bulls or took care of my own business. He must have learned how to deal with bullies long before I did.

I don't recall what Ronnie did that evening to arouse my anger to the breaking point but he was going to pay full price. I was livid. He was a rat bastard, son-of-a-bitch who enjoyed my suffering, and I'd taken all of his ridicule, pushes and shoves, and stealing of my belongings that I was going to take from him.

I wailed on him. I had never hit anyone or anything so hard. His knees buckled and he went down. Like a wounded animal he was still dangerous. It took all of my strength to maintain my grip on him, but he could not escape. I could have broken his nose or bloodied his mouth, but I really didn't want to hurt him. He wasn't a bad guy. I think he turned out to be a decent adult. But, for a while, he was a very misled child.

We were sprawled on the floor of the old high school gym that doubled as the cafeteria for the junior high school. It was Youth Night and we were surrounded by a bunch of kids our age and older. In the words of an eleven-year-old I told him that the name calling and the tormenting had to stop.

"Right now. It's over!"

He had little choice but to agree with me. I am sure his friends didn't know what had started the tangle, but they seemed surprised that the smaller Myers kid was in control. When Ronnie realized that his friends were aware that he was not as tough as he boasted, the struggle subsided. He relented and assured me that things would change.

One thing was certain. He had knocked around the wrong kid for too long, and it was "game over" for Ronnie. He never bothered me again.

I encourage you to employ your wits to avoid any physical fight. I have not been in a fight since junior high school.

Nevertheless, my father's words are still as applicable today as ever, "Apparently he doesn't like being bullied!"

Don't ever put up with a bully.

Climate Fact:

Public schools devote only 1-2 hours per year teaching about climate change. In 2023 the top news programs devote less than 1% of their air time to covering climate change. They cover the hurricanes, floods, fires and droughts but seldom discuss what makes them dangerous and more frequent.

What can you do about it?

Read on. Get educated, get mad and get active.

What I want to be when I grow up

"You can be what you think, but you are what you do."

It was dark and so cold I could see my breath form a cloud as it wafted into the amber rays from the street lamp above me. The snow, stacked from the shoveled driveways and sidewalks, was up to my waste, and it crunched like the crust of three-day old French bread as I trudged through it. The ruts on the pavement were difficult for cars, treacherous for pedestrians, and impossible for bicycles, so I was pulling a sled filled with fifty-eight copies of the Battle Creek Enquirer. I was twelve years old.

I delivered newspapers after junior high school in the winter of 1957. It was my first fulltime job. Fulltime in that I had to do it every day except Christmas. Like most twelve-year-olds in my small town, my pockets were empty, my resume was limited, and my job prospects were scarce. My father was a masonry contractor and I had often helped him, but the damned blocks weighed half as much as me. Construction work was not an option.

I kept complete records for an entire 154-game schedule of a fictitious baseball game we played that featured Major League All-Stars all the way back to Ty Cobb. That emboldened me with aspirations of becoming a statistician for the New York Yankees. Unfortunately, I was only half-way through my first year of algebra. So much for that prospect. Newspaper carrier was one of the few regular paying jobs that a twelve-year-old could get. Even it required an apprenticeship so I had to be a substitute for my cousin, Larry Myers, for an entire year before I was able to get my own route.

I was able to take over my cousin's route when he started playing high school football. The late afternoon practices conflicted with the demands of his delivery schedule. Except for Sundays, the Enquirer was an evening newspaper. I had to deliver it every day after school. It was a serious obligation, but I was thrilled! I had a job. It was like having my own business. I got paid each week so I always had some walking-around money. I had an established route and if anyone in my area subscribed to the newspaper it was assigned to me. Ca-ching! The more customers I had, the more cash I had in my pocket. It demanded that I work every day, no sick days, and in every kind of nasty weather. There are few jobs that require one to work each and every day, and I had one of those.

Sunday was the most demanding day because I had a more customers on Sundays than on weekdays, and the newspaper was twice as large as other days. I never understood that. It made me think that Sunday-only subscribers got all the news they wanted from one day of the week. What happened on the other six days didn't matter. It seemed that such a lack of interest would inevitably lead to a certain degree of ignorance. I was only in seventh grade but I knew that on the list of things that everyone desired, the bottom three were sick, poor and dumb as a board. Maybe they just wanted the coupons. Every Sunday newspaper was twice as thick as usual due to about thirty extra pages of ads with coupons. Guess I shouldn't be too judgmental. I read Mad Magazine from cover to cover. It was funnier than seeing legless frogs in wheelchairs being wheeled through the kitchen door of a restaurant that was offering a special on deep fried frog legs, but a literary bonanza it was not.

My route was slightly less than average in size. It wasn't big money, $5 to $7 each week, but it paid for the stuff I needed like bicycles and accessories, baseball gloves, bats and balls and, of course, sodas and candy bars. Yes, I had to buy my own baseball glove. Although my first bicycle was a Christmas gift, I paid for each one after that. My sister, brother and I had chores and everyone worked if you wanted more than the basics. Both Mom and Dad worked so we weren't poor, but we were frugal. If I cracked a bat, I would drill a hole through the crack, screw the pieces together and secure it with electricians' tape. That gave it a half-season more, but it made buying a new bat with the name Mickey Mantle or Stan Musial on it an absolute treat. My newspaper route assured me of those special moments.

I wasn't thinking about those things this evening. It was freezing cold. My fingers were icicles and my feet were as numb as gun-metal. I just wanted to get home, thaw out and have a hot meal. I hadn't stopped for my usual slice of custard pie at the diner next to the railroad tracks because I wanted to finish before dark. Too late for that. This evening's challenging climate had doubled my usual delivery time, and it was already pitch black.

It was not a strenuous job but pulling a heavy sled through weather this brutal hadn't come up during the discussion of the transfer of the business from my cousin to me. I was facing three more deliveries, and they were all a mile away, well beyond the E. W. Bliss factory that had stood on the edge of town for years. I wasn't sure I could make the mile down there and back. The cold was the kind that froze in my nose when I inhaled. I was miserable.

I looked down the dark and dreary highway past the Bliss factory and then turned the sled in the direction of home. I was hoping that if my mother were home from her job she would give me a ride to the last three homes in a warm car. She had done it before. I hesitated, aware that my mother, big old-fashioned bundle of love that she was, had her limit. She had to drive twenty miles each way to her job as an executive secretary for a Battle Creek manufacturing company. It would be a lot to ask her to interrupt her evening dinner preparations to help me. And I knew what Dad's response would be, "You signed on to deliver fifty-eight newspapers, not fifty-five!"

I shivered as I debated my options. It was about the same distance to home as it was to make the deliveries. If mom said "no" I would be taking the risk that I would have to go back to finish the job or forget the deliveries. Neither of my options was promising.

A story my father had once told me about one of his high school football days popped into my head. I must have considered it relevant to my dilemma.

"I played on both sides of the ball," he said. I knew that meant he played both offense and defense.

"This night," he said, "I was on defense, and their halfback had run over me for over half the game. I hurt, I was tired, and we were losing. My pride was taking a real beating." He frowned and the creases in his brow suggested his despair had been as deep. Then he added, "The other guy was bigger than me, but I didn't think he was better than me."

I don't know from whence he summoned the resolve or the energy, but as he relayed the story to me it seemed to have something to do with self-imposed limitations or self-respect. I think he was trying to tell me that I could do almost anything upon which I focused my mind and my energy. Conceive it, believe it, achieve it!

"I finally had enough.," Dad said. "I made up my mind that he was not going around me or over me again. The next time he carried the ball, he came through the line unblocked. I could see the confidence in his eyes, and he didn't try to go around me. I squared my shoulders, got low and charged. He went down hard, real hard. On his back, hard! I think it surprised him because it took him a while to get up." Dad paused before adding, "They didn't run him at me the rest of the game."

The smile at the corners of his lips and the air of satisfaction that enveloped him affected me the most. It was quiet, unadorned pride.

The only thing that stood in the way of the successful completion of my responsibility on this cold night was my attitude. As I looked again down the dark road past the Bliss factory, I imagined the aroma of home-cooked meals and the warmth from fireplaces of the homes that were awaiting their evening newspaper. The same comforts were awaiting me at my own home, and the sooner I got going, the sooner I'd be able to enjoy them. I had to finish the job.

I picked a light in the distance and headed for it. Each step took me closer to my destination. Although it was my job to deliver to those last three remote locations, they were not my destination. It was the sense of completion that drove me, the sense of satisfaction I knew my father felt after pan-caking that running back years ago. It was old fashioned self-respect that had been passed along by generations that had come before me. I was fueled by that special feeling. It drove me to overcome the coldness in my bones and any willingness to settle for less than what I could be.

On the outskirts of the city, the snow had not been plowed, the piles were deeper and the ruts were harder to negotiate. More snow began to fall as the temperature dropped, but my new resolve moved me forward. I left my sled behind, trekked to each home and made the final deliveries with almost a bounce in my step. When I got home, dinner was waiting.

"How was your day?" my mother asked.

"Never better!" I responded.

Whenever I am faced with any of the inevitable challenges that strain my limits. . .or burden my sense of well-being, I resurrect the picture of that twelve-year-old boy pulling a heavy sled on that dark, bitter night and remind myself: "If he could do it, so can I!"

Climate Fact:

Agriculture is responsible for 90% of deforestation. Mangroves and coastal wetlands hold up to five times more carbon per acre than tropical forests. The United Nations Intergovernmental Panel on Climate Change has determined that by legally protecting 30% of our land area from abuse and development is close to what the Earth needs to rebalance itself. Only 16% of land is now protected in some way.

What can you do about it?

Experts tell us we need to protect more environmentally sensitive areas. Wetlands, forests and areas that are huge carbon sinks should be protected. Do not support new development in protected areas.

Respect must be earned and how I came to love strawberry pie!

"Respect is the greatest gift you will ever receive."

The first thing I recalled when I woke up was the number 98. Or was it 97? The light was dim, and I had no idea what time it was. I was lying flat on my back. The room was cramped and included a single chair and a high stainless-steel stand that was parked next to my bed. Okay, I'm in bed. But where? I heard the sound of voices from what resembled a television sitcom. Mounted on the wall was a TV but it was not turned on. Then I realized I was in a hospital.

"Wow!" My memory was returning and what amazed me the most was how quickly the I-V had relieved me of consciousness. The doctor had said, "Start counting backward from 100," and I don't think I reached ninety-six before going night-night.

My sight was okay, but I had no idea if the surgery had gone as planned, and I was afraid to touch my face. I'd been promised stitches between my eye and my ear as part of the second attempt to rectify the injury. If you cup your hands in front of you and then slip the fingers of one hand into the other, you will form an arch that will resemble the architecture of my face before the fall. The dive from the rafters, ten or twelve feet to a solid oak floor, had sent me into partial shock, given me a black-eye the size of a kiwi and interrupted my baseball team's pitching rotation. I was their captain and the starting pitcher.

What happened? Four blocks from the center of my hometown, Hastings, Michigan, my father had volunteered to take down an old two-story building in return for the rights to the materials. There was a lot of value in used double-hung windows, hardwood planks and solid two-by-fours because they formed the structural frame for most houses. A few years later Dad would build his own home entirely from second hand materials. Among things he was a skilled and frugal carpenter. Helping him raze that old building had become my job between pitching starts during the summer that separated my junior and senior years in high school. It was 1962 and I had not yet turned seventeen.

The surgeon, with a reputation as the best ear, nose and throat specialist in the area, had just completed his second effort to reform the bones on the right side of my face. They had been rearranged by the impact with the floor. I spent one night at the local hospital and was then driven to another in Battle Creek after Mother demanded that her son be treated by the best "face guy" in Michigan. I had taken one hell of a blow to my right cheek.

The first operation, which involved an attempt to force the bones back into that arch-like shape without leaving a scar, was done by entering my cheek through my mouth. The sympathy cards and colorful blooms were giving life to my otherwise antiseptic room, but the operation had failed.

This time I expected a small but noticeable scar in the hairline along my right temple. He was going to cut me open on my face. It was there. I could feel it. Still I wondered why I didn't feel any pain on my right cheek. Of course, pain killers. One could become addicted to the kind of medicine that masks that type of discomfort. I was sure I would prefer them for now because pain is part of life, tolerable to a degree and usually temporary. I also knew I wanted to get off them as soon as possible.

My mind was racing. At age sixteen I was energetic, athletic and a quick healer and expected to be back on the mound soon. In fact, within a couple of weeks, I was repaired enough to pitch a no-hitter. But I was also as vain as any adolescent with a full hormonal palate and a hyperbolic concern for his appearance. If that second procedure wasn't successful I was facing an even more formidable scar that the next surgery would leave behind. Such a scar is like a public tattoo, noticeable and permanent. I could imagine a zig-zag pattern across my face that would become my introduction for the rest of my life. That is exactly what I was told would result if the doctor exercised the sure-fire approach, cut into my cheek and forced the bones back into place. The procedure from which I was now recovering was less certain in result and still involved a small incision that would leave a mark. After the pre-surgery meds had dissipated, my anxiety level was as high as those rafters from which I had tumbled.

The fall had been an accident caused when Dad tried to flip a long joist, with one end resting on a rafter, as I stepped across it. Bad timing! It hit me on the rear and cantilevered me into the air. There was nothing to stop my fall but the floor. Dad felt terrible, but I never blamed him. Accidents happen.

As full consciousness returned, I saw mother standing at the corner of my bed, forcing a smiling.

"How are you feeling?" she said.

I wasn't yet verbal, but I was alive and that was good. I tried to smile but it wasn't happening.

"Before long the doctor will join us," Mother said as she laid a comforting hand on the sheet that covered my legs, "and give us an update." My mother was the cheerful and optimistic sort so her lack of gushing enthusiasm suggested that things hadn't gone as planned.

The doctor didn't show up the rest of the day. We discovered he had left word that he would return the next day ostensibly after the swelling had dissipated and I had fully recovered from the effects of the anesthesia. Mother feigned patience all day and, upon leaving that evening, left the nurse in charge with a few choice words. Mother's vocabulary was colorful as the nurse learned.

Mom returned the next morning after taking another vacation day from her job as the executive secretary to the vice president of marketing for Clark Equipment Company, a lift-truck manufacturer in Battle Creek. She was an important cog in the wheel of the corporation, and taking time off created issues. She tried to remain calm, but I could see the impatience churning within her. By late morning there was still no doctor.

She checked with the nurses' station several times and each time was told, "The doctor is very busy. He is still seeing patients at his office and will come as soon as he can."

The fact that he had a patient in the hospital facing unknown consequences and a parent that had taken another payless day from her job had apparently not registered with him. That was numero uno on my mother's mind.

Joyce Elaine (Frey) Myers, my mother, was a remarkable woman. She survived five different bosses and ran the marketing department between each transition. Clark Equipment Company was recognized as the Cadillac of lift-trucks and shipped its products throughout the world. Mom was one of their "go-to" employees. As a master of organizational skills, she was called upon when the job required multi-tasking. She was a Crackerjack card player. I never saw her lose the demanding card-counting game called Hearts. Her fellow employees stopped playing with her because they couldn't win. She kept disparate things together in her job, and she was the same way with her family.

Her presence was far greater than her physical stature of five-feet and one hundred pounds. She became bubbly each time her weight dipped below the century mark. She was a generous hostess and a loving parent. In fact, in spite of her devotion to and the skill with which she approached her professional career, her family was the most important thing in her life. She was kind and very thoughtful and if you were among her circle of friends, she could make you feel, when you were in her presence, that you were the most important person in the world. She was also a Sagittarius, prone to speaking her mind before fully considering her words. Used to being in the presence of men of title and power she was never intimidated. If you hadn't earned her friendship or her respect or if you were a threat to any member of her family, it didn't matter what title or position you had attained in life. My little Sagittarian mom could turn into a viper.

As we waited to hear the specifics of my less than satisfactory surgery, mother's increasingly testy inquiries had become noticed throughout the ward. What filtered into my room was that the doctor had been about seventy-five percent successful in returning my facial bones to their pre-injury shape. It meant that a third procedure was looming. That translated into more sedation, more stress, more time off work for mother and a big scar on my face. Our tension was rising.

Mother became quieter but more fidgety. She stopped trying to comfort me with her usual clichés, "He'll be here soon, honey," or "Don't worry. Everything will be all right."

It was late morning when a nurse came to tell my mother that the doctor was still seeing patients in his office and would come as soon as possible. Mother's reaction was prompt. I suppose she didn't want to upset me, but her tirade began as soon as she led the nurse from my room to the nurses' station. She didn't call anyone bad names, but her wrath was directed at one person. Everyone on the ward was now aware that a dangerous snake was loose.

"I don't know who the hell this doctor thinks he is, but I'm tired of you covering for his ass!" Mom said. "He may be the best ENT (ear, nose and throat doctor) in town, but he hasn't earned that reputation with me. Get me a wheelchair. My son is checking out!"

"Go, Mom!" I thought. But where are we going? I'm in a hospital gown recovering from surgery and in the care of ostensibly the best guy in the biz and she's going to take me to someone else, maybe second best. My emotions were mixed, but I trusted my mother more than I trusted that doctor. And you don't mess with a dangerous reptile.

In the meantime, more cards and flowers arrived. I was surprised to get cards from two really cute girls that I didn't know were aware of my existence. I had no idea that sympathy was such an effective ploy with women. Getting hurt was not the worst thing that could happen. I made a mental note to contact them when I got home.

The biggest surprise had come from Aunt Eloise, my Mother's sister. She and my uncle, Gerald Shepard, lived on a dairy farm on the outskirts of Battle Creek, only a few miles from the hospital. She had left me a gigantic piece of homemade strawberry pie. Who doesn't like strawberry shortcake? Mother would crush the fresh berries and add enough sugar so that over freshly baked biscuits the strawberries became a heavenly treat. Strawberry pie was different. I wasn't sure I liked it. The berries were tart without sugar and made my mouth pucker. Every year in June mother would take me to the U-Pick-em farm where we would load up on enough berries to put the overflow into a freezer. It meant I would be having my favorite dessert, strawberry shortcake, for the rest of the summer. I loved strawberry shortcake. All by themselves in a pie, though, I was expecting to pucker, but it looked delicious, like something on the cover of a Better Homes and Garden magazine.

The big ripe red berries had been dropped whole into a thin white crust, glazed and topped with whipped cream. How bad could this be? I took a cautious bite. The fruity combination was like having Christmas and my birthday happening in my mouth at the same time. Instant love. I was licking whipped cream from my lips when mother rolled a wheelchair into the room.

"I had to go all the way to the first floor to get this. Let's go," she said. I began to change into street clothes.

"Change later," she said. The urgency in her voice could not be mistaken. We were leaving.

I sat in the wheelchair and mother piled my clothes, gifts, playing cards and other belongings onto my lap. I resembled a homeless person with a shopping cart full of everything he owned. I would have been embarrassed by my attire, but everyone else in this place was dressed as a nurse or a patient.

As she pushed me to the elevator that would take us to the main floor an entourage of women in white caps and starched dresses looked on in disbelief. One of them, possibly the head nurse on that floor, provided the only interference.

"Mrs. Myers, you can't go," she said. "The doctor hasn't discharged your son."

"Watch me," said Mom.

The elevator door opened. She wheeled me in and the second floor disappeared from view.

Word of our imminent departure had spread quickly. We were met on the first floor by someone with a name tag that read: Admittance Nurse.

In a civil voice she said, "Mrs. Myers, please come to the office for a moment. There's some paperwork you need to complete." It may have been an attempt to dissuade her but my mother complied.

Mother spun my chair toward the office. She was in a major league hurry. The stack of things in my lap teetered precariously, and I shifted from side to side to catch the things that were falling overboard.

The office served for both admissions and departures. It was the size of five or six hospital rooms and was filled with desks and chairs, occupied mostly by middle-aged women.

One of them said to mother, "Your doctor is the best in his field and in big demand."

Another encouraged her to be patient, "He knows you're waiting and he'll be here as soon as he gets done with his office visits."

"News travels fast around here," Mother retorted.

The rest of the conversation went like this, although mother was the only one speaking. "This guy cut into my son twice and neither operation worked. Now he's not willing to show his face or talk with me. I don't care how good he is or what his reputation may be, he can't treat us this way. If you don't get him on the phone right now we're leaving." It wasn't a request.

Someone dialed a number and handed the telephone to my Mom. Within moments my mother was telling the premier ear, nose and throat specialist in western Michigan exactly what she thought of him, what he was going to do next, and how long he had to arrive at the hospital before she wheeled me out of there.

Mother's performance had brought the entire office to a standstill. No one moved or said anything. I got the feeling that no one had ever spoken to the revered and feared medicine man in that fashion.

Mother handed the telephone to the nurse. It was so quiet the only sound was that of the handset being placed back onto the cradle. The intrigue was palpable as everyone waited for my mother's next move.

"Take us back to the room," mother said and turned toward the door. "I think he's on his way!"

I couldn't help but notice the corners of her mouth turn up when she said it. Everyone stood and applauded.

Did I tell you, my mother was a remarkable woman?

Climate Fact:

Industrial agriculture (large scale corporate farming) is destroying the fertility of the soil. In spite of all the pesticides poured upon the plants and the soil 30% of the crop is still lost to bugs and other intruders. Restoring and protecting our ecosystems, from forests to wetlands, can provide over 1/3 of the CO_2 reduction needed to prevent global warming from exceeding 2.0 degrees Centigrade (3.6 degrees Fahrenheit) by 2030.

What can you do about it?

Once again, the answers are simple for most of us. Buy local produce. Eat organically. Support efforts that foster small farms and preserve sensitive lands.

You may try to control your emotions, but they are always in command

"If you should need God it probably means you are at your wit's end. Shout to the heavens for relief! It's a terrific catharsis and it can't hurt anyone unless you violate a noise ordinance."

"Thud!" The ball hit the bat like the sound of a duck flying into a barn door. It trickled down the first base line.

I charged from the mound in a race with the batter, but the first baseman fielded the ball and beat each of us to the bag. Another easy out. Little drama here except that it was the fifth inning, and the other team had yet to get a hit.

The pitcher's mound on every regulation baseball field in America sits sixty-feet and six-inches from home plate in the middle of a slightly elevated and exquisitely manicured diamond of green. It was the same for the mound at Johnson's Field, the athletic complex for my high school, home of the Hastings Saxons. It was huge: 15-20 acres of prime real estate that was once owned and farmed by my grandfather, George Henry Myers. That's where the track and tennis teams competed, where my father played both football and the drums, and where I was king of the diamond this day.

I walked back to the mound and stood on the same patch of ground that my father once plowed with horses, a long homerun from the field on which he excelled in football. Over my shoulder, beyond right field and the clubhouse, if my grandparents were watching from their attic window, I could acknowledge them with a nod of my cap. A quarter moon was ascending in the summer sky.

I suppose I wouldn't have been there that day without them. My grandmother, Grace Myers, was a short woman with a keen wit and a bodacious smile. She was a woman of many talents but her life was mainly that of stay-at-home mom, and she was a great cook. It was more than a fulltime job living with my grandpa. She said the years after he died were the calmest she had known. I really liked her. Everyone liked her. She was Grandma.

My grandfather was an abrupt man with a crusty exterior, dry wit, and an opinion about everything. His smile could light a dark room and in his chest was a heart as soft as cream cheese. I loved him. He evolved from one type of work to another and was usually the man in charge.

At one time he ran the local post office, he was a skilled stone mason, and at another time, he had a brief career as a Realtor. Thus, I was on that diamond that day because he probably brokered a deal with the school board. Maybe he sold the property during The Great Depression of the 1930s to support his family. I know for sure that every Friday night football game for the next thirty years he complained about the traffic, noise and littering all the athletic teams and their fans brought with them.

If they were watching me with their feet propped upon a chest filled with memorabilia of Dad's feats, it would have been nice to think about rewarding them. I was pitching a no-hitter, one of baseball's greatest accomplishments, and I wanted them to beam with pride. But more important at that moment, I was only sixteen and not prone to waxing philosophically while trying to keep a wicked dropping curve in the strike zone.

I turned back toward Steve Turkal, my catcher, put my toe on the mound and waited for his sign. He kept asking for one thing and I wanted another. I waived him off so many times he called a time-out and trotted to the mound. With all of equipment he was wearing he resembled Chewbacca with less hair.

"I need to know when you're throwing the curveball because it goes all over the place," Steve said. He was a big guy and unafraid to block my errant pitches with his body, but that didn't mean he enjoyed being a human backstop for my wildness. "Make a motion with your glove when you want to throw the curve." He was trying to simplify things.

I nodded my concurrence. It was a good idea because it let me call my own pitches, but it was unorthodox. The catcher always called the pitches. That was part of baseball protocol. I understood the protocol and the traditions in baseball and complied with them. It made me part of a special club. In fact, intimate knowledge of those traditions gave me and my baseball fanatic friends real stature in this club. What club?

We were part of an informal group that played baseball, read about baseball, watched baseball and had our radio dial preset to as many games as we could pick up on our home or car radios. I could pick up Detroit and Chicago games. We got our news of the world from the Sporting News and Sports Illustrated. We played imaginary games with complete major league rosters and kept stats for an entire 154-game schedule. (Today the season is 162 games because several new cities were granted a franchise in 1961.)

We had shoe boxes full of complete series of baseball cards. Among my collection was an original 1956 Mickey Mantle card, the year he hit .356 and won the Triple Crown. Today it's worth more than my car. If mom hadn't included my baseball cards in her list of things to be discarded during one of her Spring cleaning bursts while

I was attending college, I'd be living on my investments from the sale of those cards. It's not a cliché when I say, "We ate, drank and slept baseball!"

I loved the game so much that one of my friends nicknamed me "the organizer." I could pull together two teams for a game in just thirty minutes. I'd call a couple of guys. Each of them would make a call or two, and I'd collect them in Dad's flatbed pickup truck on the way to the ballfield. I'm not sure that I even had a valid driver's license when that first began.

When Dad took me to ballgames in Detroit, it was usually to see the New York Yankees and their roster of superstars play against the Tigers. Somehow the Yankees had become my favorite team, and a Sunday double-header with the Tigers was the highlight of my summer. Even today as I drive into any large city, it rekindles the wonderful memories of those trips to the big city and Tiger Stadium.

Walt Whitman once said, "Baseball is America's game."

I say, "Get a favorite team and go to the game."

Protocol aside, my catcher had legitimate concerns that merited his idea that I call the pitch. Pass-balls are a stain on a catcher's resume, and wild pitches can leave a painful welt. I had only two pitches if you didn't count my change-up. It was slower than the other two and anyone over ten could hit it, including my sister. I threw it only to break the monotony. Of the two primary options, Steve had a preference for my fastball because it was easier to catch. Correction, it was neither fast nor straight, but at least it wasn't the second one—the dreaded curveball. I was not fast, but then neither was I consistently straight.

My go-to pitch was a dropping curve and it came with variations. It was also the one that created Steve's anxiety. One version, the three-quarter curve, would start at the right-handed batter's head and drop across the plate. Even a slowly thrown ball hurts like hell when it hits you and both Steve and the hitters had plenty of reasons not to trust my accuracy. Most of the right-handed batters bailed out. Automatic strike!

The other version of that pitch came almost directly overhead and dropped across the plate as if it were falling off a table. It was a pitch I adapted from watching my older cousin, Bruce Thompson, throw a plastic Whiffleball, and it was virtually un-hit-able. I was a little better than average as a batter, but I don't think I could have hit that pitch. Only two kids ever hit my dropping curve for extra bases, and it wasn't going to happen on this day!

The next batter was the weakest hitter in their lineup. What is true in the major leagues is true in high school baseball. Good pitching always has the advantage, and the weakest hitter in the lineup is always the last man in the batting order. To his credit he got the bat on the ball. I threw a couple of curves on which the kid whiffed before he ended the fifth with a feeble infield pop-up to third base. We had a three to one lead going into the sixth. A walk and an error in the fourth inning had led to a run.

As I mentioned baseball is a game replete with traditions. Every kid, in fact every baseball fan, is aware of one of those traditions. In the later innings of a game no one says anything to a pitcher who still hasn't allowed a hit. Our games went seven innings. There were only two innings left in the game and the other team had yet to get a hit. I knew it, my guys knew it and the other team knew it, but nobody said a thing. They weren't avoiding me, but they did everything to avoid the subject, or they just kept quiet. It's all about the jinx.

I can't say I believed in the jinx, but I respected the tradition, and being part of the club brought with it a reward. When you know the batting average and the ERA of almost every player in the major leagues the adult men in your life are impressed. They were once avid club members, but they're usually too busy to absorb that much detail. Knowledge and adherence to those traditions elevated my stature in the club.

I was not a dominant player nor was I a dominant pitcher. I probably lacked the proper disposition to be hugely successful. I wasn't demonstratively emotional as a youngster unless it concerned sports. I inherited a family trait, the discipline to suppress the same emotions that so many others expressed freely. Success, we had been modeled, was derived from intense focus, funneling our emotions and overcoming setbacks. There were no failures, only learning opportunities. When you got knocked down, you got up and hit harder, much harder! No self-pity. There was a correct time to unleash your emotions. I am still damned disappointed when I lose.

This approach is a terrific driver, instills a competitive nature and helps propel success in many endeavors. My father taught me that anything worth doing is worth doing well. I really liked how it felt to win, the reward, increased status among my peers and the intrinsic internal charge it provided. I believe this drove me to achieve a level of accomplishment that I would likely not have reached without that force in my life. I didn't just want to win that game. I wanted to dominate the other team.

That drive has its downside, however, and it was soon to illustrate that lesson to me.

If I wasn't a dominant pitcher and I had only two different pitches how could I be throwing a no-hitter? In rating the most difficult feats in sports, hitting a major-league fastball is one of the greatest challenges. The ball is coming at you faster than highway traffic and moving up, down, or away from you. Standing in the batter's box requires the confidence that you can get out of the way of a rock thrown as hard as possible at you and you have a second and a half to swing or duck. Few high school age kids possess that assurance or have overcome the fear of the rock. My curveball moved so much it made the batters duck or strike out.

In the top of the sixth, Wayne Lydy, the kind of hitter that pitchers feared, came to bat for our team. He was farm kid; not brawny, less than six-feet tall and couldn't have weighed more than 160 pounds, but he could hit a baseball a long way. There were two outs and a man on first base. Although he was a left-handed batter, he hit one over the left fielder's head. If it weren't for the chain link fence it could have rolled beyond the city limits. When Lydy touched home plate our lead had been padded by two runs. A lead takes some pressure off a pitcher to be pin point with his accuracy, but it can't do anything about the kind of stubborn tendency I mentioned earlier.

Sometimes you can try so hard to do something that it causes you to malfunction. In other words, it causes you to do the thing you didn't want to do. In golf and baseball, you are told to relax before you swing. Take a deep breath to reduce the stress of the moment. Stress creates tension, and tension causes things to break. In other words, if you can't control your emotions mistakes can occur. Combine the tension created by the prospect of a no-hitter with my stubbornness, and it will help you understand what happened in the bottom of the sixth.

The other team had still not reached base on a hit, but my wildness had resulted in two more runners reaching base with walks. My dropping curve was a little less on target than usual. When it dropped in front of the plate it sometimes got by the catcher, even one as big and resourceful as Steve.

With one out and runners on first and second, after a slight wiggle of my glove to alert my catcher, I threw the three-quarter dropping curveball. The batter stayed in the box and took a terrible swing as the ball dropped short of home and caromed to one side.

Steve moved to block it, but it ricocheted off his outstretched mitt. He scampered to retrieve the ball, but his aim was no better than mine. His throw to third ended up down the left field line. The runner scored easily and the runner from first had rounded third when the ball game into the infield. I had crossed the third base line to back up a throw to third base so I had to run back toward the mound in order to cut off the throw from left field. As I fielded it cleanly I realized that a quick throw to third might beat the runner who had taken too much liberty after crossing the bag. An easy throw to third may not have nailed him, but it would have prevented him from scoring or created a run down between third and home. The other team still hadn't managed a hit, and I doubted they would, so those two runs were tarnishing the luster of my performance. I was juiced and threw the ball as hard as I could toward third base. Big mistake: wild high! It sailed over the third baseman and another runner scored.

As I returned to the hill, I was feeling anything but proud. Nor was I thinking about my grandfather or his complaints about the rambunctious fans that disturbed his once quiet neighborhood.

"They're not at all like you when you used to gallop your horse down the streets of California towns, take it to its knees and slide through saloon doors!" my father once told him, but it made me proud to think of my grandfather as a spunky young man. That Grandpa so easily dismissed that analogy made me aware that he had already passed some of that strain to me.

If you are ever accused of being stubborn, you earned it the old-fashioned way. You inherited it. That night it caused only an extra run to score, but there are times when it can be more damaging.

Let's finish the baseball story. I struck out the next two batters and retired the side in order in the seventh inning to preserve the no-hitter. We won the game five to three. Not a lot was said, probably because such an achievement is normally associated with something closer to perfection.

The base on balls, wild throws and the three runs had erased any resemblance to that. The next week I pitched a one-hit shutout. It was the best game of my life. No one reached second base. It was a near masterpiece except for one thing. It wasn't a no-hitter.

I love this game.

Climate Fact:

Without stronger greenhouse gas emission policies, Earth (Our only home!) is projected to warm up by 3.2 degrees C (5.76 degrees F) by 2100.

What can you do about it?

Demand that every person who represents you in government make combatting global warming his or her first priority. Then, walk your talk. Get educated and take action. Become the world you want to create.

Any job worth doing is worth doing well

"Things attained through dedication and hard work are always more appreciated than any gift you will ever receive."

"Kaboom!"

The airplane exploded as it crashed into the Pacific Ocean. My father, frozen by the sight of the Japanese fighter plane heading straight for the bow, breathed a sigh of relief. Only eighteen months out of high school he was aboard a Navy hospital ship in the Pacific as a result of the Japanese invasion of Pearl Harbor on December 7, 1941. That attack brought the United States into World War II.

Thirty years later, in the early 1970s, the Japanese mounted another invasion. This one brought thousands of Japanese cars into the showrooms of American automobile dealers. Although now household names, brands such as Honda, Toyota and Datsun (now known as Nissan) were new to consumers in the United States. In contrast to American vehicles they were tiny and underpowered, but they were well-made. They should have been. We helped them build new state of the art factories after the war.

Those cars also arrived with a stigma caused by the destruction and death that my father's generation endured at Pearl Harbor, Okinawa and on the Bataan Death March during that war. There was residual animosity harbored by many Americans in regard to those imports and, if you lived in Michigan and cared about your neighbor, as we did, you drove an American car.

For my father the choice of cars was very personal. "I wouldn't drive one of their cars if it was the only one made. Those sons-a-bitches tried to kill me," were his exact words.

It was an ironic statement because I never saw him discriminate against anyone who was Japanese during his entire life. He was a man of enormous tolerance if you worked hard and were honest.

In 1945 my father, George Louis Myers (his friends called him Louie), was aboard the USS Relief, a 500-bed hospital ship that accompanied the campaigns in the Pacific as the United States fleet moved toward the occupation of Japan near the of end WW II. Dad was on the Relief when it took aboard the wounded, many of them burned in the long and bloody battle for Okinawa, and the emaciated survivors of the war on the islands in the Pacific Ocean.

Less than two years earlier he had graduated from high school and gone to Western Michigan College in Kalamazoo, Michigan (now Western Michigan University) to pursue two passions: learning and football. His aspirations were interrupted by the war. He was not alone.

Fifteen to twenty million Americans served in some capacity from 1941 to 1946. The world was being attacked on all fronts by bigots, tyrants and terrorists such as Germany's Hitler, Italy's Mussolini and Japan's Hirohito. Americans are a diverse group of people with many opposing points of view. We have our share of bigots and tyrants, but there is one thing that almost no American will tolerate: a threat to his or her freedom.

Dad shared this thirst for freedom. His unquenchable desire to live life on his terms was handed down to him through what has seemed to be some genetic code. When he was drafted by the U.S. Navy in February 1944, he was not surprised nor did he harbor regrets. It was his responsibility to serve and defend the principles that so clearly defined him. The war did, however, change his life forever.

Although he served as a tailor on the USS Relief, the deafening thunder of long-range cannons and the flow of bloody and limbless bodies across the gangway of his ship became etched into his memories. He was a small-town boy who grew up plowing fields by horse behind his home and heating stones to warm his bed during the Great Depression.

His sister said that before the war he was a happy and free-spirited soul. Upon his return he had become more somber and reserved. Most young people of college age look forward to the new horizons that travel opens for them. After the war Dad's common refrain in regard to visiting some far-off place was: "I've seen the world and I don't need to see any more of it."

It had been a sobering way to grow up quick. When he donned a sailor's uniform, he left behind his childhood sweetheart, my mother, with whom he would spend fifty-one years and raise three children. They'd dated since they were sophomores in high school. To say that Dad was devoted to my mother was an understatement. That is not to say that he was a perfect mate, the consummate communicator or romantic sort, or that he provided mother with all of the emotional support she required. He just absolutely adored her. While in high school my mother, Joyce Elaine Frey, worked part-time at Hodges Jewelry Store in Hastings, Michigan. (Her fondness for fine jewelry continued throughout her life.) She had her eye on a ring that featured the cameos of two women's faces in white set against a black onyx stone. She once told her granddaughter, Heather Rocco, that it broke her heart when she noticed it was missing from the store front window. Without her knowledge Dad had made payments on that ring for months in order to make sure she got it. She was wearing it the day she died.

The sailors on the USS Relief had been mending the wounded since its first commission in 1920. It had been attached to many military campaigns throughout the world but spent most of the Second World War in the Pacific. On both starboard and port sides were painted large red crosses to signify its status as a hospital ship and to distinguish it from a battleship. Aboard the Relief, Dad assumed, if there were any rules of civility during war one of them was that you did not attack a hospital ship.

The Relief was usually accompanied at sea by a sister ship. During one campaign the Relief was still in harbor for repairs while its sister sailed with the fleet into battle. It was sunk by Japanese kamikazes. The kamikazes were pilots who gave up their lives by crashing their airplanes into enemy battle ships, aircraft carriers and even ships that served the wounded and helpless. The Japanese leaders did not play by a rule book. During his time in the military Dad developed a disdain for war and the inhumanity that evolved from it. It may not be a stretch to say that he hated the thought of war. For a man with a profound faith in God this made sense to me.

Aboard the ship, he was assigned as a tailor to repair clothes, shoes, leather and anything else that needed mending. It was a skill he later applied, after retiring from carpentry, when he opened a shoe and leather repair business in Battle Creek, Michigan.

He believed that if your treated others with dignity and expected them to act with integrity, most of the time they would not surprise you. When he was away from the shop, he left the door unlocked and the repaired items, with invoices attached, on the shelves. His customers were instructed to leave the payment in a cash box behind the counter. Someone took his shoes without paying on one occasion, but no one ever stole a dime.

On that Pacific morning, while delivering a set of newly stitched dress-whites to the captain's quarters, he was stopped in his tracks by the sight of a Japanese Zero headed straight for the Relief. He had been trained for that situation, but he was in the middle of a combat zone and aware of the fate of their sister ship. At 484 feet, the USS Relief was half again as long as a football field and almost impossible to miss. A direct hit would sink it.

Somehow the young Japanese pilot, devoted to the service of his country and convinced that his loyalty to the Emperor would be rewarded in the afterlife, missed the ship. As Dad watched with his heart in his throat and his future suspended, the Zero crossed the bow and dived into a cold Pacific grave.

When my father relayed the story to me forty years later, his memory of that day was as vivid as the morning's sunrise. My father treated everyone with respect, was color blind and never discriminated against anyone regardless of gender or nationality. Nevertheless, he never owned a Japanese automobile. In fact, I never saw him even ride in one.

Dad seldom shared accounts of his wartime experience but I became aware that his assignment as a tailor may have been somewhat of a relief to him possibly due to the delusion he conjured that the assignment would probably not place him at the end of an enemy soldier's gun-sight. However, it was war and that was the job he had been assigned to do. Having survived the Great Depression of the 1930s meant that if you were offered a job you took it. Any job! And you did it well because there were many others around ready to step in if you were not up to the task.

I learned from him that when I perform a task, especially a paid one, my reputation is on the line. It doesn't matter what the job is. It informs others of my skills, my attitude and my ambition. However minor or seemingly mundane the job may seem at the time, it is preparing me for the next assignment and for my life.

Dad may have been disappointed that he had been yanked from college and had his football career interrupted, but he wasn't going to allow that assignment as a tailor to diminish him. When he became a tailor in the United States Navy, he resolved to learn everything about that trade that was available on a ship. He excelled at the job, exceeded expectations and earned the respect and favor of the brass aboard ship. By the time of his official discharge in May 1946, he had earned the Philippine Liberation Victory Medal, the American Area Campaign Medal and received a star for his participation in the Asiatic Pacific Area Campaign. He never mentioned any of it.

Although he seldom discussed that time in his life, his philosophy about life and work bored into me. Like most college students from middle class families, I looked for work in the summer to help pay my college expenses. Even though I was fortunate to earn a scholarship to pay my tuition at the University of Michigan, I still needed all the money I could get my hands on to pay for clothes and books and meals. Summer jobs didn't come easily, so I took what was available my first two years.

My favorite was working with the grounds crew at a prestigious private country club in Battle Creek. I disliked having to start work at seven a.m., but I got off at three and a golf course is like an oasis in the city. The aroma of freshly mown fairways, the architecture of exquisitely sculpted greens and the general civility of the environment excited my senses and shaped an appreciation that years later would turn into a love affair with golf. Besides, I got to drive trucks and tractors all over the golf course. What guy doesn't like that?

It was another much more mundane job that provided me with the opportunity to appreciate my father's philosophy of work. It occurred immediately after completion of my first year in college. I was broke and scrounging for work. I responded to a help wanted ad for labor to unload freight cars at a local lumber company. The low wage was made more attractive by the promise of a performance bonus.

My job was to transfer lumber from box cars on a siding next to a lumber yard and then onto trucks for delivery to job sites. Based upon the multitude of boxcars lined up on that track I expected to be one of a plethora of manual laborers when I showed for that early morning assignment. To my surprise, other than the supervisor, I was the only guy who showed up. The supervisor gave me simple instructions, "Get them out of there and put them over there," and departed.

It was heavy work in hot weather inside confined places, and there was no way that one man could unload all of those cars. It seemed to me that fact might put the performance bonus at risk. Without the bonus I was little more than slave labor. Upon his return, just before noon, I needed to clear up the compensation issue. The bonus, as I expected, was dependent upon getting the cars unloaded in a specific amount of time. When he told me that there would be no else to help me I realized it was going to be impossible to reach the goal. To further jeopardize my situation, he told me that the hourly wage was actually less than was advertised. I knew I could not do a worthy job for people who had lied to me. I walked off the job.

It was not without trepidation. I worried about my father's reaction. He couldn't afford to send me to college without my contribution, and I had quit a job. I was afraid he would think I wasn't up to the task or that I wasn't willing to work hard for something I really wanted. I really wanted a degree from the University of Michigan.

At home I told him about the job and the supervisor's deception. His response surprised me. He said, "Good for you!"

Within a week I found another job, one that paid more and involved working with honest people. It wasn't as important or as dangerous as being a sailor on a Navy ship during wartime, but it was the beginning of a lifetime of work and put me in charge of writing my own resume.

The message that day from my father was clear: "Any job worth doing is worth doing well."

Climate Fact:

Although China and India each have four times the population of the USA, Americans produce six times more greenhouse gas per person. We are, therefore, the top polluter on the planet.

What can you do about it?

There is good news here. Because Americans put out more greenhouse gases than other countries, we have more opportunities to reduce our collective carbon footprint. This will be accomplished by recognizing that every decision we make either aids or defeats this enemy. You are in control of your destiny.

Let your dreams be your guide

"We make the world in which we want to live."

Once upon a time I had a dream. At the time I thought the idea was original. Later I came to realize that, although its design may have been my own, the concept was an extension of the philosophy of those in our family who had come before me.

The first part of my goal was to be independent. To achieve that, I wanted to create a home and an environment that would minimize my living costs, reduce my financial requirements and mitigate my dependence upon others. That would allow me to do work that I enjoyed, work driven by something other than monetary goals. It could also be work that could empower others.

The second part of my dream was to achieve that goal while leaving the smallest possible carbon footprint, i.e., the least amount of pollution in my wake. I reasoned that if I could reduce my demand for extemporaneous and trivial consumer goods I would also reduce the trash and waste I would create. If I used alternative methods of energy production such as solar and wind, I would reduce my use of fossil fuels and the greenhouse gases they create. And I would recycle or multi-purpose most of the resources such as water and food wastes. What I sought was to create a living environment that would be healthy for me, my family, my community and most other living things on the planet.

Last, by raising my children within that environment I could teach them by example. I wasn't especially religious, but I was raised in a family with a high code of ethics, so such a goal seemed to be unselfish and appropriate.

How was my dream influenced? I was a child of parents who lived through the Great Depression of the 1930s and World War II in the 1940s. Those were times when frugality, conservation and self-sufficiency were necessary for survival. Those requirements, however, had already become traits of our family's nature.

In the Spring of 1976 the opportunity for me to achieve my dream presented itself. The story had begun 130 years earlier though, and involves the legendary Daniel Boone.

In the first half of the 19th Century, three men got out of a canoe somewhere near the confluence of the Little Miami and Stillwater Rivers. That is across the street from what is now the Dragons baseball stadium in downtown Dayton, Ohio.

One of those men was a general in the U. S. Cavalry by the name of Cooper. He was accompanied by Daniel Boone, probably because Boone was familiar with southern Ohio. The general surveyed the area and decided it would be a promising place to build a home. He did just that circa 1840 in an area that later became known as the Oregon Historic District.

Today that area has become a community of restored homes, churches and small businesses that attract a bustling night life with its attendant bars, restaurants and boutiques. For unknown reasons the house that General Cooper built was not occupied until 1860, a year before the outbreak of the Civil War.

That one hundred and thirty-year-old house, a two-and-one-half story brick double, was to become the focal point for the achievement of my dream.

Prior to 1970, the Oregon Historic District had become an inner-city ghetto. The neighborhood was home to down-on-their-luck winos, wayward sorts and low-income retirees from the plethora of factories that had dominated the inner-east side of Dayton from the 1940s through the 1960s. By 1975 it had become fashionable for younger urban pioneers to resurrect those old homes and reform the neighborhood. Some of my thirty-something friends had already invested and had begun the arduous but exhilarating process of renovating the deteriorating architectural gems.

The low cost of the homes and the financial incentives available for investment in that historic district were an easy match to my limited balance sheet. Along with the skills I had learned at my father's side during his years as a contractor, I felt that I knew how to build things. I contacted a real estate agent who showed me the Cooper House. Then, I needed the down payment.

At that time, I was developing a countywide crime prevention project, a government job. My salary was a livable one, but it wasn't enough to buy a home. That was until a life insurance annuity policy, purchased on my behalf by my parents when they were young, came to maturity. I used the twelve-hundred dollars as a down payment on the old Cooper building, and the journey began. The building had been relegated to a ten-unit rooming house with untold housing code violations. The year was 1976.

During that summer I left my job during lunch hours to meet with contractors, obtain bids for remodeling, and reassure tenants that I would give them plenty of notice before asking them to vacate the property. To most of us, it seemed they were living in squalor. To them it was familiar territory and the only home they could afford. They deserved my respect.

Because of them, the restoration of that old house was accompanied by many strange events, but one afternoon was beyond memorable. It became emblematic of what often happens when gentrification collides with a rundown inner-city neighborhood.

I'm not sure I would have endured it without an ample sense of irony and humor.

During one noon meeting, I was escorting a plumber through a unit occupied by a longtime elderly resident. He had alcohol on his breath and a revolver tucked under his belt. I knew the old guy well enough to consider him harmless, but alcohol and guns seldom mix well. I got as close to him as if I were waiting on his table in a restaurant and then pointed at the gun.

"What's that for?" I asked.

He recoiled and the gun slipped down his pant-leg. It hit the floor with a huge thud. Instant panic! My head almost hit the ceiling as I leaped to avoid being hit by a stray bullet. The gun didn't fire, but I was going to have to call another plumber. He had disappeared through the back door. The old man dropped into a chair. I picked up the pistol, took a couple of deep breaths and wondered what I had gotten myself into. All I could do was laugh.

Meanwhile, Callie, whom I called the resident mother because she lived rent-free in return for screening and supervising tenants, sought my approval to rent an upstairs room. A feeble old man had been dumped on my front porch. His daughter had driven him to this ghetto from a hospital in Middletown in what I surmised was an attempt to relieve the burden he had become for her. His vision was impaired, his glasses held together by adhesive tape, and he was bruised all over his body indicating he had been bedridden for weeks. He had all of his belongings in a paper bag and was barely able to climb the stairs to the second floor.

I was too busy to object because the heating contractor had arrived, but I didn't go into that room for several weeks for fear I would find a body rotting on the floor.

That the neighborhood had become a depository for the wayward and the infirm was apparent as the drama continued. Upon descending the stairs from the second floor I passed Callie who was now leading another lifeless old-timer to a small, dirty and dank room I had cleared out for renovation.

"No," I said to her. "That room is not available." It was so nasty I wouldn't have kept pet fleas in it. "Besides, there's no bed up there!"

After a trip to the basement to inspect the ductwork with the heating and cooling rep I returned to the front porch. Callie was waiting with a grin on her face and some cash in her outstretched hand. It was over one hundred dollars.

"What's this? I asked.

"Fifty dollars per month for the large room upstairs," Callie said.

The daughter of the old geezer had paid for two months in advance. That further confirmed my suspicion that the woman had left her father to die in my building.

"And fifteen dollars for the room in the back," Callie added.

"There's no bed in there," I reminded her.

"There is now," she said, beaming with pride. Although I was soon going to evict everyone to begin renovations she was still doing the job she had been performing for years. She was filling those rooms with paying souls.

"I got a bed from the garage," she said.

As I cleared each room for renovation I stored the old furniture in the three-car garage behind the house.

"How did you get them up there?" I asked. She couldn't carry a bed up there alone.

"A couple of bottles of port," she said and placed some small change in my hand.

Callie had traded cheap wine for manual labor. She knew most of the regular winos in the neighborhood. The rents she had collected totaled $115 and she had given me all but two dollars and fifty cents, the cost of two bottles of the cheapest port wine that would not etch the glass.

"Callie, we don't have to poison two people just to get a bed upstairs!" I said in exasperation.

They would drink both bottles within the hour and pass out. Her resourcefulness had been the source of her pride, but I couldn't help but note the irony of the situation. I was not used to that way of life.

Another time it took me thirty minutes to rouse a drunk who had gone to sleep on the front porch of my house. He was dirty, decrepit, reeked of offal and was as good as dead. I didn't want to touch him for fear his condition was contagious, as if he were a large glob of noxious rot, which with contact, would contaminate me. He was a fellow human being in need of my help, but he creeped me out.

That day was a reminder of how cheap life could become. I closed my eyes, exhaled and took a moment to collect myself.

Upon purchasing that historic property, the challenges that accompanied were obscured by my enthusiasm. I was excited about owning my first home. I was anxious to employ the semblance of handyman skills inherited from my father. And I was anxious to begin the process of tearing down and rebuilding a home that could fulfill a dream, with my own hands.

It didn't take long to grasp the biggest challenge. The old house was solid brick and had no insulation. That created a heating and cooling nightmare. The windows were aging double-hung wooden ones through which the wind flowed like smoke through a screen door. It was heated by an ancient coal furnace with an electric stoker that died during renovations in the blizzard of 1978, the coldest winter in fifty years. The aging building had multiple fireplaces but only two were operational.

The only gas supply to the building fueled the cook-stoves in the kitchens and small space heaters in some of the rooms. At that time natural gas was the preferred method of heating because it was a fraction of the cost of heating with electricity. During the Arab Oil embargo of 1973-74 that decreased the supply of gas to residential units, Dayton had been limited to that which a home had been using in the recent past. That meant my old building didn't have access to the amount of gas needed to efficiently heat it once it was renovated. I was living on limited income and faced insurmountable electric bills due to the rationing of natural gas. That was a dream killer. I needed a plan.

My interest in conservation had led me to a copy of "The Urban Integral Handbook." The book described an inner-city home in Berkeley, California that was retrofitted to reduce its dependence upon the local power and light company while minimizing and/or recycling the waste generated by its residents. It was a manual for creating an energy efficient and sustainable living environment within an urban neighborhood, and it became my blueprint for success.

"Wow! This could really happen!" I thought as I digested each page. I could retrofit my house with energy efficient windows and insulate the walls and ceiling without difficulty. I would recycle waste water from showers and washing clothes to be used again to flush toilets and irrigate the garden. Those were reasonable, doable and cost-effective items, each described for me in the book as if I were reading an installation manual.

As I read and re-read the pages of this book, my dream began to take on a real shape, but there was another huge obstacle facing me. That would be obtaining approval to install four-hundred square feet of solar panels on the roof facing the street. The panels would generate both power and controversy because my home was situated in a qualified historic district, subject to strict rules of renovation. The Historic Society required restorations to match original designs, materials and colors as much as possible. The installation of four-hundred square feet of solar collectors on a home built in 1840 clearly violated each and every one of those mandates.

I was not deterred. It didn't matter to me that it had never been done or that I didn't have the funds to complete that type of renovation. Sometimes it helps to be young and idealistic.

My pitch to the decision makers would be simple: if we don't create a model for this type of conversion, middle-class homeowners will not be able to afford these homes and our inner cities will suffer from lack of development. I used the crisis causing a shortage of fossil fuels to develop a plan to incorporate the use of solar energy in my restoration as a way to raise the necessary seed money.

Fortunately, there were plenty of stakeholders. The City of Dayton had created an independent financial vehicle to support urban home purchase and remodeling efforts. Lenders, urban planners, engineers and the Historic Society would all benefit if the plan succeeded. In fact, they would be required to sign off on the project.

One never knows when an MBA is going to come in handy. Writing a business plan was no problem, but I needed a grant. During my tenure with the Regional Planning Commission I learned to apply for funding from governmental agencies that provided start-up money for innovative ideas. I put together a detailed proposal and hosted a dinner of all of the stakeholders, the most important of which was the director of the Historical Society. Without his approval the project was dead in the water. We dined on the 30th floor of the Kettering Tower in most prestigious restaurant in downtown Dayton. Two hours later the engineer had convinced the Director to recommend approval of a plan that would provide the necessary equity to finance my dream. Upon completion I would become the first person in the United States to have installed solar collectors on a multiple family residence listed on the National Register of Historic Places.

What they didn't know they didn't need to know. Once the building was converted from a rooming house to three apartments, the cash flow from two rental units would cover the mortgage payment. The solar system was designed to cover the costs of heating the house and the water for bathing and dishes. My family could live in the larger unit without the burden of a home payment. In addition to a small electric bill, my only other costs would be insurance and property taxes. I had a plan for handling those costs, too.

The home had a spacious attic. It was large enough in which to stand upright. By employing a drip irrigation system in the attic, I could grow a small cash crop of cannabis for my friends through the use of hydroponics. The revenue would cover the fore-mentioned costs. That development never came to fruition, but if one is going to dream he should dream big.

It was as close to self-sufficiency as I could become and the realization of a dream that would lead to financial independence. Unfortunately, a mere twenty-four hours before the closing of the mortgage loan on the house, a mechanic's lien was slapped on the property by one of the suppliers to the solar panel installer. It took eighteen months to remedy that situation, a timeframe in which the economics of the project were changed. Five years after acquiring that historical structure I was able to complete the renovation, but I was able to enjoy the fruits of my efforts for only a few months. My life and my finances required that I move out and move on. The fulfillment of my dream would be delayed.

I knew that Thomas Edison didn't invent the light-bulb on his first attempt nor did the Wright brothers get off the ground in their first airplane. It has been said that Elder Beerman suffered nine bankruptcies before achieving his dream of operating a chain of department stores. Elon Musk's rocket-ships still collapse on the pads, but he is still going into space. Achieving the stuff of dreams is difficult. It's supposed to be. Perfection is valued and rewarded. Sloppiness is not. Perfection takes time, often a long time, and a lot of "practice, practice, practice!"

How long? I began playing golf when I was sixteen. It took fifty-three years to achieve my first hole-in-one. It took only three more years to get the second one. Then, for the first time in those fifty-three years, I shot under eighty during two consecutive rounds of golf and eventually whittled my handicap to below ten (if only for one month). If you can achieve one really important, spectacular, fantastic thing in your life, you will have succeeded more than most, but it may take an entire lifetime to do it.

Your great grandfather, George Louis Myers, made it clear to me: "Any job worth doing is worth doing well." He was a very talented man who spent his time doing the things that brought joy to him and to others.

Stubbornness can easily attach itself to bull-headed and misguided ambitions. So, from time to time you may have tweak your goals. That's okay. If the goal is worthy, can be achieved while you take care of your obligations, and it benefits others, it will be worth the sacrifice. Of course, there will be sacrifice. A lot of it! The wonderful and awesome part is that as a result of your sacrifice, you will be generously rewarded. Life offers many types of rewards, most of which are not financial. The pursuit of dreams that add something beneficial to the human experience provides the greatest reward because it results in the satisfaction of a job well done. The pursuit of those dreams often serves as a motivation to others. There are those who will follow you, so dream big!

Once upon a time I had a dream. I still do!

Climate Fact:

The lights, phones, computers and appliances you leave on while not in use contribute to global warming and add 25% to your home's utility bill.

What can you do about it?

What are you thinking? Turn off idle lights!

If I Can't Live Forever, Get Me to 100

"If you don't have a goal, you'll never hit it."

I've always set goals for myself. When I was in my thirties, I decided I wanted to live to be one hundred.

Silly me! Little did I know how rare that was. In 1950 only 2300 people lived to be one hundred years old. By 2021 over 87000 people had reached that ripe age. By 2054 it is predicted that 3.5 million of us will become centenarians. Still, that's only one tenth of one percent of the population. To put that in gambling terms, the cards are definitely stacked against us.

I ignored the odds and did a little research. I discovered that three things would be required for me to reach that milestone. First, I had to choose my parents well --- genetics. Second, diet and exercise. Third, environmental factors.

I was blessed that my ancestors lived long and healthy lives for the most part, but there was nothing I could do about the first factor. Number two was definitely under my control, so I went back to school to learn everything I could about proper diet and exercise. One of the traits most often equated with longevity is VO2 Max, a measure of strong lungs. I started running but due to the shock to my body, I took up bicycling. For years I rode over a hundred miles every week. At age seventy-nine I still ride twenty to thirty miles each week and spend a couple hours in the gym lifting weights.

When I began studying our environment, the third factor, I discovered that we are polluting our air, water and soil, the very things we depend upon for our survival, to unsustainable levels. Generally speaking, those who live close to mines and factories that produce toxic waste products suffer from cancer at a far greater degree than those who do not. Their air, water and soil are more likely to be tainted with life threatening chemicals. This reminded me of the lesson I learned about ecology while fishing with my grandfather. However, it never occurred to me to write about it. It would take three seemingly unrelated events before I felt impelled to put what I learned on paper.

The first of these events occurred in 1990 while I was driving along coast of Lake Michigan. On the radio a representative from the Michigan Department of Natural resources was taking calls from listeners. An elderly woman asked, "How many tumors are normal in the big fish in Lake Michigan?" I had spent hours fishing from the piers off the coasts of Holland and Grand Haven in my youth. We always caught our limit of fresh water perch which mother lightly floured and pan fried into the sweetest treat I have ever tasted.

The young man from the DNR interrupted the caller, "Madam, madam, It's not tumors. It's tumor," not wanting to alarm listeners. In recent years Lake Michigan had become a mecca for larger game fish like coho salmon so the lady's question was of great concern if it was true.

She raised her voice to the level of a stern warning, "Sonny, you're not listening to me. These fish are full of tumors." Later I discovered that she was correct.

Not long after that I relocated to Tampa, Florida. Within a three-month period in the early 1990s two small articles appeared in the local newspaper. The first reported that one thousand American white pelicans had dropped dead, like fodder from the sky, onto the ground around Lake Apopka in central Florida. Unlike the brown pelicans that are common from Florida to Texas these are migratory birds that herd and corner their prey in the fresh water lakes of Florida and other warm winter States. This had never before occurred.

Like the first article only one column inch was devoted to the second one which reported that ninety percent of the alligators around the same lake had died. Wildlife experts indicated that their reproductive organs had shriveled up to the point they could no longer reproduce.

In a relatively short period of time three separate incidents involving the deaths of large numbers of three different species had occurred. For someone with a great connection to and appreciation for wildlife this hit me like a mallet to the head. Call me crazy, but I frequently talk to animals. I consider them friends. What would life be like without other animals? I had to find out what was causing these deaths.

I looked for the answer in scientific journals and environmentally focused magazines. Then I contacted the Florida Department of Natural Resources. It was to no avail. I called the folks at the Natural Resources Defense Council and the Audubon Society. I got hints and innuendos but no one would definitely point to the culprit. I had my own suspicion, but it was a few years later that I found the answer: pesticides. These chemicals had been sprayed upon the orchards of Michigan and groves of Florida for a long time. Along with industrial run-offs these poisons washed into the nearby lakes and poisoned the food supply for the birds, fish and alligators that depended upon them for their survival. This was occurring from coast to coast. Once again, I realized that not only was my grandfather correct, this was occurring on a national scale. I had to write about it.

While writing my first novel, appropriately entitled Pest, an ecological thriller, three children were born to farm workers in North Carolina and Florida with horrific birth defects --- one without arms and legs, another without a jaw and a third died. Two national supermarket chains had to stop selling the tomatoes from one grower because he had violated pesticide regulations 88 times in Florida and 369 times in North Carolina. Simultaneously, the Canadian government reported that the over use of pesticides was leading to lower IQs in children. The mis-use and over use of pesticides, herbicides and artificial fertilizers was polluting the water and the soil everywhere. My concerns were being substantiated on a daily basis.

The use of fossil fuels and chemicals by large scale industrial farms was ruining the soil and polluting our air and water to unsustainable levels. The only way for me to reach 100 was to exercise as if my life depended upon it, eat only organic grains, fruits and vegetables and stay away from toxic locations. I gave up milk, sugar, salt, refined white flour, deep fried foods and red meat. If it came from a four-legged animal it wasn't going into my mouth.

At age 79, after not spending a day in the hospital since college, I was diagnosed with pancreatic cancer. For most people this is a death sentence. The doctors who successfully operated on me said that the only reason that I qualified for the surgery and that I recovered so well was due to my previous health habits. Developing proper diet and exercise habits could someday save your life. We now know it is also healthy for the planet.

Climate Fact:

If the cement industry and its products were an independent country it would be the 6th largest emitter of greenhouse gas on the planet.

What can you do about it?

Build your home with wood and steel whenever you can. Building with wood and steel, instead of concrete, reduces fossil fuel use almost 20% and CO2 by over 30%.

The things you have to do to get a job

"The harder you work, the luckier you will become."

"You want me to come over there and kick your ass?" the stranger snarled as he approached.

The year was 1978. It was one-thirty in the morning and that reprobate and I were the only people on Fifth Street. All that illuminated me and my Chinese egg-roll cart was a small overhead spot-light, a distant street lamp and the rays that filtered through the windows of the saloons on the other side of the street. I was at work in Dayton's Oregon Historic District. Everyone else I knew, including my children, were home and tucked into their beds.

The stranger's eyes were glassy. His tie was in disarray and half of his shirt was hanging out. I don't know whether he had been fired from his job or the last woman in Newcom's Tavern had dismissed his advances, but the alcohol had etched a scourge into his face. One look at me and he'd decided that punching out the food cart guy would somehow elevate his status.

I doubt that my appearance suggested that I was someone not be be "fucked with." I wore a captain's hat, a button-down white Oxford dress shirt, a blue bow tie and suspenders that sported our flag's colors. My long hair and full beard framed a business-like face and my fit but scrawny legs evoked little fear beneath my frayed denim-shorts. My costume was designed to add some theater to the nightlife in the Oregon District and to pump up sales. It worked. A lot of guys wanted to work it just to meet women. For me it was a cash cow. I used it to finance my dream house in the District.

The stranger was a big guy, outweighing me by forty pounds. He was clearly big enough to think he could kick my ass, but there was a problem. Being abjectly besotted will numb one to reality, and underestimating one's opponent is a sure way to find yourself face down on the pavement. I was having an excellent night, business was brisk, and this wasn't my first rodeo. I was Joyce Myers' boy. I ignored his taunts and stuck to my job.

"What can I do for you?" I asked as if I were the friendly clerk behind the counter of your local Seven-Eleven.

"You're a real smart-ass," he said and grabbed a handful of duck sauces I kept in a can on top of the cart.

As he flipped through the sauces the alcohol weakened his knees. He lost his balance which jostled the cart.

The cart was an old fashioned three-wheeled bicycle with an ice cream freezer box in front. I filled it with Chinese egg-rolls and dry ice. It had been extended to accommodate a deep fryer, a sink and a propane tank. Hovering above it was a red and yellow umbrella with Chinese Egg-rolls stitched into the canvas. I had several carts in my modest enterprise, but this one I referred to as bicycle capitalism.

To catch himself the drunk put one hand too close to the deep fryer. "Son-of-a-bitch!" He yelled and slashed the air overhead to cool his hand. He formed it into a fist and scowled at me. He was right on the verge of making a really big mistake. I didn't want to get into a physical altercation, but I knew it wouldn't go his way.

A quick glance up and down the street told me that no one was coming to my aid. Damn! Only twenty-five more minutes and I'd be out of there. I operated the cart from 9:30 p.m. to midnight on Wednesdays and Thursdays and until two in the morning on the weekends. It was the most fun I'd ever had on a job and I made more money from those four nights than I did on my day job as the chief accountant for a home improvement company. I was offered anything I needed by my fans, friends and customers who brought me beers, food and weed. They occasionally stayed around to talk about relationships, sports and politics. The time between customers was spent listening to a baseball game or smooth jazz from an NPR station on my portable radio.

In spite of the benefits of the job it came with risks. With tired legs and smelling like scorched peanut oil I had to peddle the cart home each night down dimly lit streets with a wad of cash secured only by a small padlock. And sometimes, like tonight, there were the customers from hell.

I had never gotten into a fight with a customer. With an apron full of loose change and a deep fryer full of scalding grease there was too much at risk to let it happen tonight. I stiffened my resolve and readied my best weapon—my wit.

You may be asking, "How does a former commercial banker whose input was sought on multi-million-dollar loans wind up on the street hawking munchies to disgruntled losers in the middle of the night?"

"Imagination and necessity, my lad," is my answer.

Our family has been endowed with intelligence, a work ethic, good health and a persistent demeanor. We have been postmasters, general contractors, restaurant operators, farmers, liquor store owners, chefs, school teachers, bankers, real estate agents and CPAs. Each of these requires the discipline to set one's own agenda and follow it. We like being in charge of our lives.

Including the days as a street vendor, I have operated my own business for over thirty-five years. Like the rest of the family I am happier calling my own shots. I don't thrive where the marching orders come from someone else. Taking orders from someone means that they determine the agenda. Taking orders means I have to work someone else's hours, voice their interests, even if they are contrary to my own, and be subjected to their preferences and prejudices. And if I do all of that, I can only advance at their pace. That's not who I am or we are.

I suspect I am not unlike most of our family. My pride has been too great to accept incompetence and my mouth quite ready to criticize if I disagree. I was terminated from three of the first five jobs I worked after earning my MBA from Bowling Green State University. The Vice President of a large bank told me that I was the most qualified person in the division but the bank wouldn't promote me because of the way I dressed. Even though my work was exemplary and I had saved the bank hundreds of thousands of dollars by uncovering fraud, they preferred mediocrity to a turtleneck sweater under my suit coat. I suppose becoming a charter member of the National Campaign to Impeach Nixon, the sitting president during an unpopular war, also irritated the bank's upper crust. I felt redeemed when "Tricky Dick," as President Richard M. Nixon became known for the crimes he committed, resigned in disgrace.

I took my ideas to improve the banks' track record on environmental quality directly to the president, leaping over layers of management in the process. All of those things apparently suggested they could not control me. Being dispatched from a job that I really enjoyed and at which I was highly skilled created a huge challenge for me and my family. No one likes being dismissed, but I had never wanted to work for an organization that was that myopic. My competence was never an issue. Each time I was terminated it was due to my unwillingness to go along with the program and their political agenda.

My anti-establishment sentiments were actually anti-war, anti-discrimination, and included opposition to those that supported companies that polluted our environment. I was influenced by my father who was sickened by war, outraged by racial prejudice and thought that so much poverty in such a rich country was inexcusable. During my college years, the 1960s, our country got mired in the War in Vietnam. That war put my life, and the lives of millions of young men that were subject to the military draft, at risk. It also asked us to kill people on the other side of the world we didn't know for no reason we could find worthy. Almost 60,000 Americans were killed in that tragic affair along with millions of Vietnamese. The controversy brought young people into the streets in waves of protest, including me, and created an enormous political divide in our nation. I didn't oppose serving my country. My father had been a loyal and decorated sailor during WWII. Your grandmother's father, Robert Merrill Jacoby, lost his life in that war. I believe we should be able to pick and choose the war in which we want to die. For me it wasn't going to be that one. As a result, I opposed the people and organizations that supported the war, and there were many.

That decision and others raised the ire of many in positions of authority, but I was not alone. It was a time of great discontent with the status quo. Along with millions of others, I opposed behaviors and policies that were polluting our environment, and I celebrated the very first Earth Day by tacking a huge sign onto the wall in our office that entreated people to take notice of the need for conservation. One of the bank's VPs took it down.

That battle continues today even though the leaders of 200 nations, supported by the CEOs of hundreds of corporations, have signed an international agreement to reduce the actions by humans that are contributing to a destructive world-wide climate change.

I rallied behind those marching in the streets in support of equal rights for minorities and women and the dismantlement of the counter-productive war on drugs. Control over what one puts into his or her body should be a right written into our Constitution. Such an amendment should also include the right to marry whom we want, give birth when we want, and to choose how and when to die. Battles such as these, particularly the war on drugs, had become a proxy for those at war against a culture of people seeking peace and justice. I joined like-minded organizations and spoke my mind.

I was young, highly educated and brash. I was not diplomatic. Experience eventually taught me that a good idea and favorable intentions are not enough to foster change. In someone else's employ, winning ideas must further the interests of immediate superiors. Those ideas require the nurturing of layers of management above them before they bubble to the surface. During those turbulent times when rivers were burning and lives were at stake, I had neither the patience nor the inclination to wait for the faint at heart to get with my program. I expected the organizations for whom I toiled to grasp the significance of conservation and equal opportunity because, as Bob Dylan was telling us, "The times they are a changing!"

Change was slow, and I often found myself looking for another job. The rote response to my search was, "You are the most qualified person we've interviewed, but we don't think you'll stay with our company." Either they knew something that I didn't or the acceptance of mediocrity had become widespread.

I was not used to losing and finishing second was frustrating. I didn't understand why in the hell there were so many companies settling for second place? I was a hard-working, stable guy with a family to support. I could help them and they said no. I had no idea that I had become part of national phenomenon.

During that time I was interviewed by a PhD candidate working on his thesis about competent people being fired for no good reason. He told me what I had experienced was becoming an epidemic in the mid-1970s. It meant that company rosters were filled with less than the best people they could find. The best people were apparently going somewhere else or doing something else, maybe starting new businesses or inventing new products. The old, staid companies were resisting change. The 1970s became a decade of industrial decline for the United States as a result.

I had to ask myself, "Why would I want to work for that kind of organization?"

The most important reason was that I was financially stretched out, and the lack of a regular paycheck was placing a burden upon your grandmother. She had custody of your mother and your uncle, and they were counting on me to do something.

I didn't set out to become self-employed, but the continuing refrain from my friends was simply, "Spencer, you should work for yourself!"

Becoming an entrepreneur was not my primary purpose when I purchased two food carts on bicycles for $300. I thought the old-fashioned ice cream carts would add charm to the historic district in which I lived. As it turns out, it commenced a highly profitable business based upon food carts and led to five years in the food service industry.

A brief stint as the head night cook for a gourmet vegetarian restaurant led me to open my own restaurant. The restaurant was to feature a sit-down menu while people drank beer and watched old movies. Over fifty people invested in my theater/restaurant but it was stymied by a moratorium on liquor licenses in the neighborhood. The business could not succeed without that license so I returned everyone's money and closed the doors.

In the process I lost the dream home that had been the collateral for the loan that financed the restaurant. Another setback. My futility-streak wasn't as long as the Chicago Cubs, who hadn't played in a World Series for 63 years, but it was severely challenging my generally positive attitude.

With five years in food related enterprises I marketed my credentials to the restaurant industry and was offered an opportunity to join the management team of a national chain. Before long I was let go because the manager of one of their restaurants thought I lied about a bout with insecticide poisoning to spend a weekend with my children. The company knew that they were a priority for me. The poisoning was gut wrenching but worse, I was looking for a job again.

The job search had become a tiring and fruitless process. For the first time in my life I was not sure what to do. What I knew was that I was not going to settle for something that was not meant for me. It was a matter of integrity. I had to be able to give one hundred percent to a job or I couldn't do it. I would not mislead a potential employer with false enthusiasm. I don't believe in coincidences but what happened next changed my life.

In the early 1980s, an acquaintance named Sal, who was an employee of a former business partner, had become a reputable counselor in the field of nutrition and food supplements. I suggested that he write a column on the subject for the local newspaper.

I had a friend who had done a similar thing during the early days of the CB radio craze. Although he knew little about Citizen Band radios, at the encouragement of his girlfriend who was also a newspaper reporter, he began writing a weekly column that was a response to questions provided by readers. Within a few months the column was appearing in forty newspapers. It earned him enough to fulfill his lifetime dream. He moved to Florida with his girlfriend and lived on a sailboat while they explored the world.

In spite of my encouragement, Sal was reluctant. That made me wonder if there was a real need for the advice and if anyone had done it. After four weeks in the library, having perused every major newspaper east of the Mississippi river, I came to two conclusions.

First, no one had written such a column, and second, there were a lot of fat and unhealthy people whose habits were driving up the cost of health care for companies all over the United States, to the tune of billions of dollars. There was an even greater need than writing a health column. Large companies, the kind that manage their own health care costs, would be looking for people who could reduce the health risks of their employees. The street light in my head turned green. This was about more than a job. There was a new career awaiting me. I rolled up my sleeves and went to back to school.

During the next nine months I earned the equivalent of a Masters Degree in exercise physiology. I topped it off with a Certification as a Fitness Program Instructor. It was the first such Certification offered by the American College of Sports Medicine. I was becoming part of an entirely new profession. I quickly became a consultant to the fitness and wellness industry and was hired by one of my clients to manage his facility. My new career was blossoming, but time was marching forward.

With my children approaching high school graduation I explored employment beyond Dayton for the first time since moving to the city in 1969. I had assembled an appealing resume and found myself being courted, as in wined and dined, by companies out of state. When I entered the banking business in 1969 I was the first MBA the bank had ever hired. I enjoyed the prospects they envisioned for me and the attention that was paid to my progress. It was exhilarating to once again experience that kind of attention in the workplace.

When my career in banking ended, I was displaced. Dayton had been a manufacturing town, home to makers of auto parts, appliances, tires, cash registers and all sorts of things. There were no other banks in search of my talent and the manufacturing base was shrinking due to foreign competition. The principle local job prospects I could muster were the ones that I created. With new credentials and my children nearing high school graduation it was time to move on.

It's really difficult to separate from people you love, so leaving Dayton filled me with ambivalence. I had stayed in the community because my family needed me in their lives, and I wanted them in my life. The children were looking at college and they would need my support.

I took a job in a new city and spent the next four years in the fitness industry helping people become healthier. That became a springboard to the establishment of my own company. The fitness industry is largely about sales; the sale of hope. It is the only industry whose business model is based upon the failure of its customers to achieve their goals. That virtually assures a degree of turnover in customers and personnel that would break most companies.

So, I developed a program for the operators of fitness centers that would increase retention and profitability. It was successful, but the club operators were usually too unsophisticated to properly implement the program or the specialists they hired were too arrogant to comply with it. Thirty years later people are just as fat as ever and the fitness center operators haven't changed as much as flea's spit.

Fortunately, each experience is a learning opportunity and I learned about sales. It does not come naturally. It is a learned skill. Within a few years I parlayed that new skill with my MBA and developed a successful electronic payment processing company that I have operated for over twenty-five years.

What I have learned is that successful people do what the unsuccessful people won't do. They learn, they adjust and they go where the business is. They also use their heads, not their fists.

I was prepared to confront the drunk in front of my food cart with force, if necessary, and I would prevail as I had with the bullies.

But the use of force is too easy, too dangerous and totally unimaginative. I scrambled to catch the condiments that he had knocked off the cart when he fell onto it again.

"Careful!" I said, this time more sternly.

"Screw you," was his retort.

My reflex could have been, "Get your act together, buddy, or there's going to be trouble," but I chose another approach. I let out a deep breath and relaxed. My hands fell to my sides. Only the cart was between us.

"I'm guessing you haven't had a great day. Is there anything I can do for you?" I said.

I have often been amazed at how much tension can be alleviated with the expression of even a small amount of empathy.

Not this time!

"Ffff you," he spit out. His hand came at me so quickly he lost his balance and tilted backward off the curb.

A couple of thirty-ish guys who were approaching the cart with money in hand stepped close enough to break his fall.

"Watch out," said one of them.

"Get your hands off me," growled the drunk, his hands flailing at the stranger behind him.

The taller of the two winced and let out an "Ooooh" as he passed in front of the drunkard's breath. They let him drop onto the street.

"You motherfu . . .," his cussing trailed off as they turned and faced him.

They wore suits and ties relaxed at the collar but looked as if they spent more than ample time in the local gym. From the expression on their faces it was clear that the drunken man might want to choose his next words carefully.

All eyes were upon him. Even in the stupor that had engulfed him he must have recognized the odds, one against three. He mumbled something unrecognizable as he regained a semi-upright position and wobbled away.

"Thanks," I said to the interveners.

"Obnoxious chump. He was thrown out of Newcom's," the shorter of the two said. "You have to deal with this every night?" asked the other man.

"Fortunately, not," I said.

"Two eggrolls, please," the tall one said and held out a five.

"It's on me," I said, handing each one a hot, delicious Chinese eggroll.

As the drunk turned the corner I added, "The things you have to do for a job."

Climate Fact:

Producing energy for homes and businesses using solar and wind energy is now less costly than fossil fuels. Utility companies are raising rates 6-8% per year. 80% of the materials used to make solar panels are recyclable. 95% of the materials in batteries can be recycled.

What can you do about it?

This is a no brainer! You cannot recycle coal or gas, and their by-product is CO2 (Carbon Dioxide). Replace your utility bill with a smaller monthly payment for a solar installation. This will get you off carbon and create a hedge against inflation. Note: Don't buy a home without a south facing roof.

Pick a sport and it will reward you

"Take up golf if you are short of frustrations in your life."

"Crack!"

The sound alone told me that Mac had parked another one. That cannon shot was still rising when it passed the 404 sign in dead centerfield. Another patented Mark McGwire home run, and I was there to celebrate history in the making.

In the steroid-filled Major League baseball climate of 1998, Mark McGuire and Sammy Sosa were competing to break the record of sixty-one home runs in a single season. The record had stood for thirty-seven years and the previous record had lasted thirty-four years. It's a fete so rare the next man to do it would become one of only three human beings on the planet to hit, at least, sixty home runs in a major league season. Think about how many men, women and children have played the game during the past one hundred years. Of the millions of people who have put on the spikes, only one has hit sixty-one in a single season.

The Florida Marlins (now the Miami Marlins) were hosting the St. Louis Cardinals in a night game at Pro Player Stadium (the name of the park at that time). The anticipation surrounding McGwire's appearance hadn't escaped a generally apathetic south-Florida fan base. The Marlins couldn't draw water in their home park, but tonight the house was full.

I may have mentioned it, but I'm a big baseball fan. In anticipation of that night I'd ordered tickets in advance. I resented the half-baked fans in Miami because the loyal people who knew and loved baseball, those of us who'd attended enough games to become recognized by the vendors behind home plate, had to sit in the upper deck for this event. The generally apathetic homeboys wouldn't have known if a mile-wide meteorite was headed directly at our planet, but they were fully aware that Big Mac was chasing a meteoric event in baseball. Still I was happy to score two seats behind home plate in the second deck. I had an unobstructed view of the entire field.

It was a typical south-Florida evening, warm and humid with a slight breeze drifting in from the Atlantic Ocean. It was the kind of atmosphere that could assist balls hit into the air, but this wasn't a hitter-friendly park. The walls down the line in both right and left fields were 340 feet from home plate and higher than the fielders' heads. You had earned your keep if you had hit one out of Pro Player.

That should make you aware of Mac's power. That home run, his 55th of the year, was like a rocket being launched from his bat. It came in the top of the fifth. By the time the Marlins had come to bat in the bottom of the inning, the buzz in the crowd had subsided and the part-time fans were heading for the exits. Tomorrow was a work or school day for most people, and they had gotten what they had come to see: a Mark McGwire home run. He had provided each parent and child a thrill they would share forever. For me that was not enough. I had come for a more memorable reason.

Since I was five-years old, barely tall enough to crack eggs into a frying pan on our kitchen stove, I had been a New York Yankees fan. It was a bit unusual because I was growing up in Michigan, home of the Detroit Tigers. But I wasn't the only youngster living in the aura of Mickey Mantle's fame, the Yankees' legendary center fielder. He was a sports hero to millions of people in the 1950s and 1960s and he held the record for home runs hit in World Series play until 2003.

During his playing days, he became the most prolific switch hitter in the history of the game, won the Triple Crown twice, and raced toward one of baseball's most enduring records: the home run mark of 60 set in 1927 by the George Herman "Babe" Ruth, undoubtedly the most famous baseball player of all time.

Ruth had also been a Yankee. I rooted for Mickey and the Bronx Bombers and they rewarded me with a highlight reel of good times. Trips to Tiger Stadium to see my heroes play, the aroma of hotdogs wafting in the air, and the cold crunch of Stroh's chocolate-coated ice cream bars were among the highlights of my summers.

In late August of 1961, the anticipation at Tiger Stadium was similar to the game at Pro Player. Although Mickey Mantle was having another spectacular season and my favorites were running away with the American League pennant, the spotlight was on a new hero in the making.

His name was Roger Maris. He had been a reliable but unspectacular player and a decent outfielder who had come to New York in a trade with Kansas City. Even though he was in the propitious position in the line-up of batting ahead of Mantle (Maris batted third and Mantle cleaned up) no one expected him to be chasing immortality so late in the season. No one! Maris and Mantle were neck and neck in a race to conquer Babe Ruth's record.

I don't recall the exact inning. I don't recall who was pitching or which team won the game. I don't recall any details of our trip to Detroit that euphoric Sunday. I don't even recall seeing the giant four-story rubber tire, erected outside Detroit as an advertisement for some tire manufacturer that stood as a landmark along I-94 for decades.

It was also common for my Uncle Stanley Thompson and his son, Bruce, to accompany us on those trips, but if they were with us that day I don't remember.

What I recall was the sound. The explosion that resulted from the bat hitting the ball. It overwhelmed all of the other memories of the day, and it was like the sound I had just heard as the ball collided with McGwire's bat. That crack! Like lightning splitting a tree. There is no other sound like it.

To possess the athletic focus and power necessary to do that is the unrealized dream of most young men. Men who reach those heights can become almost immortal, certainly super heroes to baseball enthusiasts.

The ball rocketed into the sky as if it had been launched toward an orbit. As it climbed it seemed to suck the air from the ballpark as well as the breath from all forty-thousand of us. It wasn't just another homer into the hitter-friendly ballpark at the corner of Trumbull and Michigan Avenue. It was Roger Maris' 56th home run of the year, and it landed in the upper deck, what my cousin Bruce called the Nosebleed Section. Maris had almost hit it over the roof and out of the ballpark. At that moment I knew, everyone knew, that the guy, about whom most of us had known only from television and the sports pages, was destined to break the most revered record in baseball, if not all of sports. We knew we were witnesses to history and to a feat that would be honored and chased for years to come.

With it would come despair and controversy. If anyone was to break the Babe's record, most people wanted it to be Mickey Mantle. America had won the war, the middle class was thriving, and we loved our heroes. We needed heroes. Mantle was preferred to Maris for that role. Maris had come from nowhere, having never hit close to forty before that season, and many thought he didn't deserve to claim the record. Mantle, the hard-drinking playboy from Oklahoma with batting titles and World Series rings, was their choice over the clean-cut Maris

The collective spite was enhanced when it took Maris an extended season to accomplish the record. Eight games had been tacked onto the season since the Babe's playing days, due to baseball's expansion and the need for more revenue. The animosity became so intense that Maris received death threats from some insanely stupid people, clearly not real baseball fans.

Maris finished the season with sixty-one. That was still the record when Big Mac came to Pro Player Stadium that late summer night in 1998, thirty-seven years after one of my most glorious summers ever. McGwire sat on fifty-five as I waited like a kid on Christmas Eve for his next at bat. Could he do it again, one more time, hit number fifty-six, just like Maris did on that summer day in 1961?

Two innings later the crowd had thinned, but there was a perceptible buzz as McGwire approached the plate. The Marlins sent in a new pitcher to face him, oblivious to the futility of such a move. Of course, it didn't matter. The superhero always prevails. Once again, he made that sound, that crack! It probably shook nearby buildings and aggregated instrument panels in passing airplanes. It was like a laser in flight over the centerfield wall and rammed into the seats a few feet from his previous shot. It was like lightning, it happened so quickly, and we were stunned. The air was electric and it hovered over the ballpark long after Big Mac crossed home plate.

I reclined in my seat, digested the warm south-Florida air, and allowed the moment to seep into my soul. Fifty-six, exactly what I had anticipated. I don't know if there was another person in Pro Player stadium that had seen Roger Maris hit number fifty-six, but on that night this middle-aged guy had become a kid again. There are still some heroes.

Within a few weeks Roger Maris' record would be surpassed by Mark McGwire's 70th homer, a feat no one ever thought could happen. At the end of the season I felt blessed. The satisfaction of having been present to share two such important moments in baseball history was almost beyond description.

Pick a sport. Play it. Support it. It will reward you.

Climate Fact:

Air travel is responsible for 9% of greenhouse gases.

What can you do about it?

Take a bus. Take a train. Drive an electric car. Electric cars require almost no maintenance, plug into your media and they are as fun as a Disneyland ride!

Stories to tell your grandchildren

"Knowledge is power, but traveling and experiencing other cultures can be as important as a formal education."

"Crash!"

It wasn't so much an accident as I had steered the Harley-Davidson into the ditch, but I was definitely down. When we hit the basketball-sized rocks, the bike and I collapsed like the 1929 stock market.

I had run a little high into an S-curve and to negotiate the turn-back I decelerated onto the apron, expecting to slow enough to slip through the curve. I had forgotten that most high-desert highways have no aprons. I was into the ravine so fast the image of the two bronzed, hard-bodied gals in the open showers next to our camp was still fresh in my mind.

Now I was asking myself, "What the hell was the rush to leave?" I was on the trip of a lifetime riding a brand-new Harley-Davidson for a loop around the country, 10,000 miles. Today I was five thousand of those miles away from home at the bottom of a ditch in northwestern Nevada. It was three days after Labor Day in 2002.

After crawling from beneath the motorcycle, a quick inventory of my body parts suggested I was in one piece except for the obligatory scrapes and bruises. If one rides a motorcycle he must expect to fall down.

My most embarrassing moment occurred in 1989. I dropped a Yamaha Virago 800cc in the dealership's parking lot. It was my first motorcycle in twenty-two years. Guess I was a little rusty. What an amateurish move. If I could have disappeared into a crack in the concrete I would have. But if you fall off your horse, even an iron one, you have to pick yourself up, get back on it and ride away. Bikers don't have a "bad boy" image because they're unshaven thugs. They're tough as nails.

This time I was more stunned than embarrassed. As of this writing I am seventy-one, shooting golf in the low 80s and looking forward to each day, but that mishap occurred fifteen years ago. I've always maintained excellent physical conditioning to the extent that most people under-estimate my age by ten years so I was surprised to discover that my reflexes had already depreciated. Other than discounted theater tickets and 10% off at some restaurants there are few positive things I can say about the benefits of aging.

It is a delight to be healthy and in a position to re-imagine the freedom I had in my youth. There is always responsibility but the most creative urges are accessed when one is relaxed. Stay healthy. It is your most important responsibility to you and humanity.

I attribute my youthful genes to my mother. She was about five feet tall and seldom weighed over one hundred pounds. She looked terrific and wore her optimism on her sleeve. The Myers were generally short and medium build. I assumed the Frey traits to be longer and leaner.

Since my thirties I have known that I would live to be one hundred years old. Grandma Grace Myers lived to ninety-six and my uncle, Robert Frey, recently turned ninety-seven. There is longevity in both legs of my family, but to live an entire century with unmitigated vigor I knew I would have to take care of myself better than the average person. In my late thirties I studied nutrition and exercise physiology and graduated from the first class of the American College of Sports Medicine. I knew that if I kept up a healthy lifestyle by using the proper diet, exercise, and stress management tools I'd acquired I should be kicking for a good long time.

None of that preparation had kept me from the bottom the ditch. Fortunately, several folks stopped their cars and scurried to my side. A couple of guys helped upright the bike while others offered medical aide.

That didn't seem out of the ordinary since I'd always answered the call of the distressed, but I was very grateful. Their response was indicative of the character of those people with whom I had shared the past four days. You couldn't leave the Burning Man Festival without being affected.

Three guys pushed the bike from the quarry-sized ditch onto the highway while I realigned myself to a new reality. I had run into a bed of craggy rocks at thirty miles per hour and probably damaged the front end of my new Harley so badly that I couldn't ride it without repairs. The nearest motorcycle shop was probably in the next state. I was stunned and in a damn big pickle of a situation.

I climbed up to the two-lane highway that overlooked the desert mesa behind me. In the valley below, a quilt of color danced on the sandy floor, woven by the thousands of revelers in the park.

In all other directions the landscape was as stark and foreboding as a remote planet with a heat index of 125 degrees. Sand and rocks, sand and rocks, stretched as far as I could see. In any other week that Nevada high-desert locale would have been a fearful place to run off the road.

With help, I reshaped the handlebars to drivable form and put a rogue lamp into one of my saddle bags until I could find a repair shop. I had yet to determine if the motorcycle was road-worthy.

"I'm okay. I'm okay," I repeated. Convincing the good Samaritans that I had regained my composure was easier than overcoming my own dismay. I take pride in my riding skills, but I had just run off the road.

Another indisputable fact was that the bartered beer, free weed, and bare bodies had intoxicated me. The women taking the public showers should have come with warning labels: "Don't operate heavy machinery after viewing!"

Unseen, ahead of me on the highway, an arrow shot straight north. Bef was nowhere in sight. On his BMW 1200 he was as quick as a fast-draw artist and as nimble as a gazelle. After four days of tent life and sleeping on hard pack, he was as eager as I was to breathe some fresh Oregon air, so he had left the Burning Man festival in a hurry. I was almost sure he would return. The guy had a law degree. Sooner or later he would realize that his riding buddy wasn't just straggling behind him. Then he would double-back to ascertain my fate.

Steven Befera was a true friend and my riding companion from Miami. We had just spent four extraordinary days at the sixteenth annual celebration of the Burning Man Festival which begins on Labor Day weekend. It had been the brainchild of seven very creative, freedom-seeking souls from the hippie generation. It retained its roots as an arts fest but had outgrown its original venue on the streets of San Francisco in the late 1990s. So much so that by the time the 35-foot-high wooden icon of the Burning Man was set on fire to conclude the celebration, the Black Rock community had become the fifth largest city in Nevada.

For me, that was the last day of a destination that had been on my calendar for months and in my mind for years. I had wanted to go to Burning Man since my best friend north of the Mason-Dixon line, Stephen VanHecke, had described it to me fifteen years earlier. I now know that you cannot walk, run, ride or fly away from Burning Man the same as you entered it. It becomes part of you and you become part of it. It is a place where one is free to express himself and there is little one can imagine that is not there.

We arrived by motorcycles during a trip that began in Miami, Florida. Upon our arrival at that barren desert playa, I said to Bef, "Bet we won't see any synchronized swimming." He laughed. I was wrong. About the only thing we didn't encounter at Burning Man was a naked Sushi Jazz bar.

Wardrobes ran from elaborate to skimpy to optional. Theme camps were common, often taking days to construct, and eroticism was favored. The result was a stretch of landscape onto which a civilization had been imposed that appeared to have emanated from Alice in Wonderland, alien planets and X-rated movie sets.

Camps ranged from makeshift tents and wooden platforms with multiple stories to metal sculptures with moving parts and spectacular light shows. All vehicles that moved, when on the playa, including bicycles, mopeds, cars, motorcycles and skateboards, required a theme or decorations.

The scene was ingenious, bizarre and beautiful at the same time. In its midst, a small group had choreographed an aquatic production without the pool, thereby resulting in synchronized swimming. The irony of it amused Bef and me for days and left us with the realization: If it can be imagined, you will probably find it at Burning Man.

Before the altercation with the ditch, we were leaving Black Rock City, 7,000 feet above sea level on an ancient ocean playa in northwest Nevada. The land on which the festival was held is managed by the national park system. That's a job I'd volunteer to do anytime. All the art, humor, free beer, and T & A one can digest for ten days. The environment may have been primitive, but it was civil and it was like salve for my soul.

The Burning Man festival was guided by ten principals which included honesty, artistry, freedom of expression, environmental sensitivity, imagination, peace and a retreat from gaudy commercialism. I also appreciated the integrity with which the founders stuck to those principles. As one participant recanted, "It's the way life ought to be for, at least, one week each year."

We had to have a ticket to enter, but we were welcome as long as we embraced the guidelines and one other thing: self-sufficiency. We had to haul in everything we needed for survival for a week because there was no commerce.

Besides no convenience stores there was no fast food, no televisions and no indoor plumbing. There were no street lights, but it was completely safe. The event was chaperoned by Park Rangers but they stood back like dance judges and intervened only to offer aide, like when one of the women in the open showers needed someone to wash her back. What made the event so compelling was that in spite of the absence of crass commercialism, the norm in American festival life, I could get a cold beer from the Tropical Cafe any day. Why? Because bartering was encouraged. In my saddlebags I stowed several edgy T-shirts from the 2002 Daytona Beach Bike Week to trade for what I needed.

Looking back, it was an oversight, but neither of us had requested a mini-fridge when we bought our motorcycles. So, unless you arrived in a fully equipped RV, you wouldn't taste a cold drink for the week. A big hoorah for bartering and for the proprietors of the Tropical Cafe for their generosity and compliance with the esprit de corps aroused by Burning Man. I traded a T-shirt for a cold beer after the playa dust had caked in the back of my throat. What a relief. What a place!

The setting for the Burning Man fest was one of stark contrasts. The sky was crystal blue and void of any visible pollution. The terrain, when it wasn't hosting the Burning Man, was untamed and free of human development except for a two-lane paved road that passed by the parkland. Cross country treks off that road were treacherous. The place was barren and the park system was obliged to keep it that way. Except for bodily fluids—and port-a-potties were provided for that purpose—we were required to take out whatever we brought in.

During the Burning Man event the parkland had been laid out in the shape of an arc with the Burning Man structure at the center of the base. It was god-like, a throwback to the times when primitive cultures created gods to worship for things they didn't understand. The streets represented meridians on a map. Each street provided a clear view of the huge, wooden icon.

At night the desert was extra-worldly under a canopy of a zillion stars. Fires were only allowed on camp-stoves and in controlled pits until the festival finale when the Burning Man was set afire in a glorious tribal blaze. It was so magnificent I imagined that people could spot the flames from their patios on the Moon and, after glancing at their cosmic time pieces, observed: "Ah, the first week in September. Must be the Burning Man festival!"

Burning Man, under the blazing desert sun, can loosen your mind and your inhibitions. Nudity is not flaunted but clothing is optional. Imagine my delight in discovering otherwise garden-variety bank secretaries, dental hygienists and salon operators strolling the playa wearing only a smile and their sandals. Although I was infused with values acquired from growing up in the basement of a Baptist church, I knew great art when I saw it. The female body, well maintained, has always been one of my favorite art forms. On the other hand, I was a whole lot less enthused by the sight of underfed, bearded, middle-aged men traipsing through the community wearing only their flip-flops. Art is, of course, in the eye of the beholder.

Night on the playa was akin to being on the set of a Stars Wars movie. Characters moved about in long robes with hoods that made them appear faceless. Shadowy figures roamed with lamps attached to their headbands. The music was acoustic, percussive and primitive. We arrived late in the day and by darkness the rhythm of the drums had aroused my most primal desires. It was eerie but exhilarating. I felt aroused, curious and slightly timid, like someone about to explore the unknown, but I never felt threatened. I sensed I was in a safe place.

Leaving, therefore, was filled with ambivalence. Four days of frolicking on the playa was slipping from view when the ditch and I collided. Once the bike had been rolled onto the highway the mist of sand upon my studded leather seat reminded me that I had inhaled more than my share of playa dust. That dust had been the primary motivation for our departure. The green pastures of Oregon now beckoned our arrival.

My image reflected off the chrome of the Harley-Davidson, and its jet-black sheet metal, dirty and dented, still glistened under the noonday sun. Up the road there was still no sign of Bef. For a moment, I felt as if I had been stranded on the Moon.

I pushed the bike forward as a test for road fitness. Nothing rubbed or rattled. I took a long, deep breath. Now for the crucial test.

"Varoom, varoom! Potata, potata," was the retort of the V-Twin after one turn of the ignition. It was as sweet a tune as I had ever heard. The 1450cc twin cam vibrated with the rhythm of the Earth. As the engine purred, my heart rate dropped twenty beats per minute.

Then the sight of Bef approaching allowed my apprehensions to evaporate like everything else in that arid climate. Finally, the day was looking up. I had never been to Oregon, and I would have enjoyed visiting my cousin, Bruce Thompson, who lived in Portland, but his home wasn't on our itinerary. I issued a heartfelt "thank you" to all whom had helped, waved goodbye and headed north just as Bef was arriving on his BMW.

"What the hell happened?" Bef asked. The bent bars and missing light couldn't be overlooked. "Are you okay?"

Bef was smart, witty and came fully equipped. So equipped that I nicknamed him Backup Bef. He had secondary systems for everything. He also had a stern and disciplined demeanor, but beneath his sergeant-like exterior was a heart of soft cheese. I'd ride anywhere with that guy.

"Much better than my bike," I said. "Let's go to Oregon." As we pulled away I said, "I need to call the closest Harley dealer before nightfall."

Why do I describe this adventure in such detail? Most people's lives, as was mine, are replete with kids, spouses, jobs and responsibilities that are major roadblocks to such a journey. The previous spring, when Bef had asked if I wanted to go to the Burning Man festival, I was intrigued. My obstacles were simple. I had a business to run and a house that required my attention. Other than that, I was available.

Then he added, "Burning Man will be just a leg in a ten-thousand-mile loop around the continental United States of America."

We had met for lunch and were sitting in his law office on U.S. Highway 1, across the street from the University of Miami. He was a Miami law school grad, but Bef was also a fellow Big Ten alum, having graduated from the University of Minnesota. I found his intellect, Midwestern directness and "hard work pays off" themes similar to my own, but it was his craving to be free, to live as if his life was his art form, that cemented our relationship.

"You want to ride, don't you?" Bef asked, well aware of the fondness I had for the open road. The grin on his face was that of a five-year-old who had been left alone in a candy store, and he was inviting me to join him.

What he was describing involved seven to nine hours per day on a Harley-Davidson living the biker life. We would camp out most of time with the exception of a few well-planned big city stops. It wouldn't be just another trip. It would be an adventure, an exploration, and it was the kind of trip one usually could take only when he was really young, really old, really rich or moving from one boxcar to another.

I was fifty-six, could probably put my business on cruise control for a while, and I had a friend who might take care of my house while I was gone. He used to be my chiropractor, and he needed a place to stay while recovering from an injury that had temporarily sidelined his practice. Dr. Jack, as everyone call him, and I used to ride and party together when I lived in the Florida Keys. He had issues that would lead to his early demise, but he was a good friend. I thought the adventure could happen.

When Jack agreed to stay at my house for the duration of my journey the anticipation fermented. Crossing the country atop my new Harley-Davidson Heritage Softail Classic would allow the sun to kiss my face and color my brow. The wind would gently caress me. The rhythm of the V-twin would nourish my soul. And most of all, although you were yet to be born, I would fulfill a lifetime commitment to myself: Make sure I have stories to tell my grandchildren.

Bef's enthusiasm was easy to appreciate since it mimicked my own. Riding arouses an intimacy with nature, and it excites all of my senses. I looked forward to feeling life without air conditioning and to be heated only by the sun. Be it cold and rainy, muggy and oppressive or hot and dry, I looked forward to waking up and going to sleep with the elements each day.

For instance, it was 109 degrees in Death Valley at six p.m. when we arrived at the north rim of the canyon. We didn't sweat. We evaporated. It was forty-seven and drizzling when we departed Duluth in August. It made us appreciate the heat of the prairie. And the change from T-shirt to leather jacket weather as we ascended through the canyons of Zion National Park from a Utah prairie was enervating.

On this trip there would be no headphones, stereos or top forty radio stations. The music would emanate from an Ohio meadowlark, the trickle of a brook beneath an Idaho bridge, and a waterfall gushing down a Yosemite mountain pass. We would taste the sweet but tart air as we passed the paper-pulp mills in Georgia and Tennessee, and we would mainline the oxygen-charged freshness of a southern Oregon meadow. We would be warmed by a Yellowstone geyser as its mist drifted down upon us from a crystal blue Wyoming sky.

I have traveled to Canada, Mexico, the Caribbean Islands, Europe, Russia and western Asia, but no place is more satisfying than this huge country of ours. On this trip I was humbled by the ancient, towering redwoods as I glided down the Pacific Coast Highway in northern California. Herds of Bison, grazing on the high Wyoming plains, transported me back to the wild west of one-hundred and fifty-years ago. Men in khakis with tackle boxes, angling trout from pristine Idaho streams, beckoned me to a simpler life. With such space to cover, I had time to create and eliminate ideas, and come to some general conclusion about the really important things in life. It is the type of journey that helps simplify one's priorities.

It was during that trip that my son called to tell me that he was buying his first home and asked if I could help him with the down payment. Of course, I would. I was as thrilled for him as a father can be.

I could have taken that trip in a car or a truck or even by rail or bus, but on my Harley-Davidson, packed high with the necessities of life, I would feel and smell each place I visited. I would interact with people in ways that would indelibly etch my memory. However, the call from my son about his new home would become one of my fondest memories of the trip.

As expected, the ride was like food for my soul. The surprises, the things I didn't expect to see, would become my dessert. I didn't know how standing upon the exact spot where General George Custer made his last stand would absolutely chill me. The brochure told me that Custer was an honored soldier, bold and brave, but my history lessons had also shown him to be arrogant, a flaw that was probably responsible for his fate. There is a lesson to be learned there.

The site of his last stand is a high spot on an open prairie in western South Dakota surrounded by a wrought iron fence. Wind-blown weeds and a few gravestones make up the terrain. It is unspectacular unless you are familiar with what happened there. Standing upon that bluff, I could sense the fear that each of his men must have felt that day. In the valley below, on the banks of the Little Big Horn River, ten-thousand Indians had amassed to make the famous general pay for his past sins and the broken promises of our country. The Indians from many nations had joined together to address the failed treaties and slaughter of their ancestors for generations by the white men. Custer and his men had no idea of what was about to occur. I could sense their fate.

When I was eight-years-old I watched a man on a motorcycle collide with a car while I was waiting at an intersection. It was the first time I had seen someone die. After college I was standing only feet from a man who collapsed from a heart attack while waiting in the teller line at my bank.

I had experienced people dying in my presence, but I had never felt death as near as it was at that moment upon that ridge. It must have been, at least, ninety degrees but I felt as if I had entered a frozen food locker. It was the kind of cold that causes your entire body to shake. High upon that bluff, vulnerable on all sides, I could hear the shrill war cries through the cloud of dust kicked up by thousands of Indian ponies along the river below. Each one of the cavalry following Custer's orders that day would have heard them too and known that they were outnumbered by forty to one.

The greatest fear in my life is loss of freedom: the ability to do what I want and when I want to do it. What I felt at that moment was fate, inescapable fate, death-like fate. I stood and shivered, chilled to the bone.

That wasn't the only time I was so affected by the threat to my unquenchable lust for freedom. In South Carolina, as I passed the remnants of old southern plantations, I could hear the haunting cries of the tortured souls that served as slaves on those lands over one-hundred and fifty-years ago. Traveling those roads attached a visceral quality to history, one that I could feel in my gut.

The idea to take this much time off from your life, to take a journey or to venture far from the ordinary, may seem unrealistic or out of reach. It may require putting some things in your life or some of your goals on hold for a while. It may take you out of your mental, physical, financial or emotional comfort level. But these opportunities are rare. I cannot express it more succinctly. When they present themselves, do not ask, "How?" Ask, "When?"

When someone asks if you would like to see the Hoodoos in Bryce Canyon (Utah's jaw-dropping rock formations) or the five-thousand-year-old trees in the Bristle Cone National Forest (the oldest living things on the planet), ask, "When do we leave?"

If you want to pass under the shadow of the four-story high recreation of Paul Bunyan, the giant fictitious lumberjack, you'll have to go to the source of the Mississippi river in northern Minnesota. Ask, "When do we leave?"

If you wish to see stalagmites and stalactites in the making in enormous underground caves a mile below the surface, enthusiastically say, "Yes, I'd love to go to Carlsbad Cavern."

If you want to understand the land and the times of Judge Roy Bean, the fictitious character brought to life by Paul Newman in the movie, "The Life and Times of Judge Roy Bean," you'll need to spend some time in the flat, dusty oil fields of West Texas, somewhere around Pecos. Just say, "Let's go there." The motto for the movie was: "If there wasn't a Judge Roy Bean, there should have been!" Riding through that place made the life of cowboys at the end of the 19th century more real for me than any Hollywood movie could have ever done.

Between Pecos and San Antonio on I-10 is a forty-mile stretch of windmills. How ironic that in the fossil fuel rich state of Texas lies the longest stretch of alternative and sustainable energy in the U.S. See it if you can and maybe you will conclude as I did that sustainable energy sources are viable.

You probably won't see snow in Snow, Arizona, but it's worth passing through that small town to get to Low Hole. I had lunch and a cold beer in a bar there. Near the bar on Main Street is a small park with two bronzed cowboys seated at a poker table. The card game, legend has it, was to decide which of the men, the largest ranchers in the area, would take title to the other's ranch. Apparently, they had come to the conclusion that the town was not large enough for both of them. Their egos had grown as large as their estates, so they played a single game of stud poker to determine the fate of their spreads. The winning hand went to the man with the Low Hole card, and the town kept the name.

The studded leather seat of my motorcycle couched me with a perfect view for my trip, and the 2002 Harley with its fat tires, refrigerator-sized windshield and saddle bags large enough to carry Imelda Marcus's summer shoes provided a silky-smooth ride.

It wasn't easy giving up something I had created, a work of art, even if it was a motorcycle, but due to a premonition, I had traded my sleek, easy handling, customized 1986 Harley-Davidson FX and its $3000 paint job for the new bagger while at the Daytona Beach Bike Show the previous March. I was sure that the bike's big easy chair, quiet belt-drive and exhilarating rubber-mounted power would soon be needed.

One call from Bef was all that was needed to fulfill my premonition. My response to his question about seeing The Burning Man festival was simply, "Hell, yes!"

When someone asks you if you would like to see the world, may you also be guided by this philosophy.

"Of course. I want to have stories to tell my grandchildren."

Climate Fact:

By 2050 the weight of the plastic discarded into the oceans will be equal to the weight of all the fish in the ocean.

What can you do about it?

This one's easy! Install a home water filter and stop using single use plastic containers. But, if you must, recycle the item.

To know love, know yourself

"Never let fear inhibit love."

This is the part where you expect to get a full dose of philosophy about love. I'm talking about the kind of wisdom a man of seventy-plus years and multiple relationships ought to be able to proffer.

You should expect it to emanate from a man with intimate knowledge of the female physique, the subtle curves, the soft touch, the gentle voice and all of the marvelous differences from what we know as male. It would, without doubt, be insight from a man with an endearing admiration and respect for women. And it should be sage guidance from someone who has never lost his desire for the excitement of romance. Indeed, I can talk about that and I promise to get into it soon.

First, let me tell you some things about a much more intriguing subject. Let's talk about sex. Even if boys don't talk about it obsessively it is the impelling topic for young men. In fact, it is for most men. Testosterone-filled and hormonally charged, most young men are loaded and ready to fulfill their genetic mandate, that evolutionary directive of all living things, to sow their seeds and assure the continuation of the species. Love, the most important and complex of human emotions, competes poorly with the basic of all human drives: pure lust. So, what I am going to tell you is likely of significant importance to your life.

There seems to be a gene in the DNA of some of the Myers men that has imbued us with a humungous sexual appetite. I mean the blazing, raging, never-ending hot kind. Not an uncontrolled or destructive fire that is offensive or abusive to women, but a continual burn, always ready to propel lift off. It persists as a constant desire, satiated only in spurts, and only by voracious lovers willing to share their passion.

Is this good or bad news? Sex is a powerful driver of behavior because it is primal. Primal to the degree that our entire species is dependent upon it. Sex is also a bonding agent between lovers. This gene, largely responsible for my never-ending carnal hunger, has fueled my urge to mate but it has unfortunately seldom led to lasting bonds. This was neither positive or negative, but it has been a part of my life with which I have had to negotiate. It may well be part of yours.

Some people are blessed or cursed with extraordinary levels of sexual energy and when people with different levels connect it can create stress in a relationship. Will this be a major challenge in your life, balancing this gene and the prime mandate with your emotional needs? And how do you even know if this gene or this characteristic was passed to you? Read this story.

One sunny summer Michigan afternoon I was fishing from a small boat with my cousin, Bruce Thompson. Bruce was three years older than me and he had already been married with a child. I was not yet twenty and, as it will among young men, the subject of sex came up. He told me that our dear grandmother, Grace Myers, had been clear about our grandfather's prowess or, at least, his oversized libido. She declared, "He can't keep his hands off me."

It was difficult to picture my grandfather chasing my grandmother around the house in her overly sensible Grandma shoes, but Grandpa was apparently highly charged. I had no idea whether he had passed that zest to me, but it was encouraging news. My grandparents had been married for fifty years and now I knew that one of the Myers men had not lost his love or his lust for the woman in his life.

Later I discovered that I shared Grandpa's passionate side. Has this been passed to you? Maybe. What does it mean? For one thing, it creates a challenge to balance the need to obey your lust with the need to have rewarding relationships. Hopefully you will connect with people who share your passionate demeanor. Choose your mates wisely because here's what you are up against.

Fifty percent of marriages result in divorce. I believe that in spite of the devotion that young lovers may have for each other and the sincere promises made to each other, some vows are difficult to keep. To have and to hold each other forever and to forsake all others is part of the addiction of romance. It is luxuriously rewarding. We become drunk with the allure of unconditional love, love forever and for all time. We often delude ourselves or just forget, at a time when our hormones and sexual drives are at their peak, that it may be almost impossible to keep such a vow. And if possessed by this Myers gene it can complicate your life.

For most of my life I have been a loyal lover but not always a contented lover since the physical need constantly demands attention. This has been a challenge in my life, maybe the challenge of my life, the balancing of my sexual energy with my emotional needs. They are not always the same, and I am certain that a difference in the levels of passion contributed to the dissolution of some of my relationships. When people become unhappy they find ways to get their needs met. I don't think men or women should remain miserable when their good intentions don't mesh with the realities of their circumstances. Try as you may sometimes people just have to move on. That happened to me more often than I desired.

What I am telling you is that sex is not the easy part of relationships. Sex may or may not come in concert with passionate love or even an enduring love, but if you get the two together it's as close to Nirvana as you'll ever come. It etches a smile on your face and adds a bounce to your step. Such love is euphoric. It lightens you and makes you feel as if you are floating upon the clouds. It also calms you while boosting your pride, empowers you and can even instill a sense of invincibility.

When it's good it's better than having your birthday, Christmas, and a trip to Disneyland every day. To know in every cell of your body that regardless of what challenge you have faced on any day, waiting for you is a place of refuge, the one person who can mend your wounds, soothe your soul, and renew the joy in your heart. And she does it unselfishly. When you can do that, too, love is like magic. In the darkest of times the two of you together can create a place where the sun always shines.

That describes some of the best that love can bring to your life. At times, however, it is a fickle emotion and the source of our greatest heartbreaks and our deepest emotional scars. It can even lead to a lifetime of resentment. You can conquer the world with your lover by your side or you can lose everything from your shirt to your home when it turns sour. That's a wide spectrum of outcomes. Some guidelines to help you know when it is real versus imaginary would seem to be in order. My sage advice: "Know your number."

Let me explain. I've been in love many times or so I thought. I've been married and divorced, more than once. During my longer-term relationships that eventually came to an end, my spirit was never dampened, nor was I sidetracked from my goal. For me, success in the form of a stimulating, passionate and enduring relationship with a beautiful gal, was to result from my ability to go from failure to failure without loss of enthusiasm. I maintained a positive state of mind, and I never stopped learning from my disappointments or mistakes.

Everyone wants to fall in love, and I have always been committed to the notion that there was someone in this galaxy with whom I could share my quest for freedom, my lust for life, and "my life is my art-form" philosophy. I knew I would meet someone who determined her own schedule and lived life on her own terms, similar to me. I was certain I would meet someone who was as content on the inside as she was beautiful on the outside. She would be generous with her devotion and as loyal a lover as me. An unflappable optimism was helpful and each potential mate was like trying on suits to find one that fit every unique contour of my being. However, there was more to it than that.

Positive things happen in our lives when we are ready for them and usually not before that. I had to be ready to give love, receive love and know that the person in front of me was truly my match, my lifetime mate. So, I came up with a practical guideline that I could correspond to a number.

Over the years I have fallen in love with a some very unique people, each with special qualities and with whom I expected to share the rest of my life. Each of them I hope would say the same about me. However, there was usually something missing. A successful relationship requires honesty, intense passion, emotional maturity and a deep understanding of who we are, our essential natures that are the driving themes in our lives. This demands that we become honest about our own nature. We need to become aware of the driving force in our lives, possibly identified by some theme to our lives.

For a long time, I was like a used car with a For Sale sign in the window that read, "Good body with a reliable engine, but has a loose steering wheel." My relationships kept bouncing off the guardrails. I had to figure out what I was doing wrong.

Psychologists have confirmed that a common ingredient in almost all long-term relationships is passion, the kind involving an intense physical and sexual connection. This connection creates both a physical and an emotional bond between people, as if they were chemically linked to each other. If something were to cause them to part or the bond to break it could cause pain.

I know about that pain because I have suffered gut-wrenching breakups, the kind that physically hurt. They involved the kind of pain I imagine an addict must feel when withdrawing from something that had propped up his life, something upon which he had become dependent. During some of those breakups it was as if an internal organ had been ripped from my body. It was difficult to breathe without pain. At times it left me unable to focus upon my work or anything other than the daily functions that were perfunctory, the ones that required minimal or no concentration. That part of what I thought had been a loving relationship, was no fun. It sucked. And it often took months for me to regain my equilibrium.

That pain eventually motivated me to figure out a way to determine whether more than our body parts were compatible when a I met a woman to whom I was attracted. I had to become aware of what was truly important to my life, the unwavering things, the deal breakers. And I had to learn to express them without fear of loss. I had to be able to communicate what I needed from the woman in my life without fearing that she might walk away if I laid it all out for her. Why had that become such an issue for me?

I feel as if I may have inherited a set of guidelines, possibly principles, through which I filter decisions in my life. They involve fairness, justice, open-mindedness, hard work, loyalty and a few other things. Almost every decision for me involves some thought to the environmental consequence of my behavior. If you despoil this environment you are messing with my wellbeing. Then came the Vietnam war. Faced with conscription in the 1960s I was faced with a life and death choice and I wasn't alone. Millions of us had to make a decision to choose to put on a uniform, get on an airplane, and fly half way across the world to kill another man for no worthwhile purpose. I was fortunate that deferments had been granted to married men and then those with children. That wasn't fair but it kept me from going to jail. I would not have gotten on that airplane.

So, like so many others, I thought I should be allowed to make all of the important decisions in my life. Whether and whom to marry. When to have children. What to eat and smoke (An entire counter-culture found marijuana acceptable if utilized competently). When to give birth. When to die. We do not have control of when we enter this world but restraining our right as to when and how to leave this world seems completely absurd.

These should be basic human rights and they were not. I cannot understand why they are still being debated today. Most people I know have enough on their plate trying to manage their own lives. Why in the hell would anyone want to take on the task of running other people's lives? But such is the nature of many people.

I've always envisioned a world of people living in peace. There can be no peace without justice and these abuses insert a level of intolerance I can't abide. I was opposed to the philosophies, policies, and people who supported these abuses.

Why is this important and what does it have to do with successful relationships? I had to acknowledge the obvious: the woman in my life had to be compatible with these principles. If I was in a relationship with a woman with whom I could imagine a long-term involvement, I should have determined if we were on the same page about what mattered the most to me. It didn't matter how faithful or devoted we may be to each other. If we didn't appreciate and accept each other for the most important ideas in our lives, our days together would be minimal. Not completely understanding the importance of this and not expressing this simple concept became a major obstacle.

There was another problem. It was my tendency to want to help the wounded. I was a child of the 1960s, a Hippie sympathizer who believed that we could all somehow get along if we showed caring and passion. It may have been a marvelously Utopian ideal but it was not enough to create a lasting relationship. We can be supportive and tolerant when people have challenging problems to overcome, but we cannot fix them. People have to fix themselves. And if we can fix them, there is no guarantee that our reward will be a forever grateful and loving mate. It is more important to fix ourselves first. Upon achieving some emotional balance in our lives and after being able to really appreciate oneself, we still have to settle upon a number.

Yes, one must have his own number. It's one you may share with others, but awareness of this number is indispensable if you really want to be happy. I am not referring to your girlfriend's telephone number, a lucky number that won the lottery, one that rolled up in a dice game or something derived from pseudo-scientific numerology.

Each of us comes into a relationship with a set of files filled with our family history, religious faith, education, ethnicity and experiences. The contents of these files are unique to each person. A substantial difference in age between mates may also have an impact. We must not tolerate intolerance, but we must tolerate the differences that make us who we are. Furthermore, we must be willing to accept and often appreciate that thing that annoys us about another person, as long as it is not a deal breaker. I call it knowing your number.

This is how it works. You have meant a wonderful gal. You feel emotionally and intellectually matched. You are filled with passion, the kind where you can't keep your hands off each other. You have been caught within the clutch of love or, at least, romance. Each of us, however, has an image, a kind of picture in our minds, of our ideal mate. Since no one person can meet 100 percent of our expectations or the picture in our mind of that perfect mate, we need to determine what percent of those expectations is necessary to make this love the sticking kind. The kind that stretches but holds together.

Is it 75 percent or 83 percent or a whopping 97 percent? I'm not talking about compromise or settling for someone who is not compatible with you, but I guarantee that if your number is 100 percent, you will be bound for disappointment.

Why? None of us is 100 percent, and we cannot expect it from another person. Your number represents the percentage of acceptance of your mate's personality, behavioral, financial, ethical, sexuality and the other life-defining traits, below which you will not be compatible. This is a number below which is a deal breaker, a no-go, a losing proposition and a waste of valuable emotional capital. And she has to become more than comfortable with your number, the one she has set in her mind.

Below this number you may try to be compatible but it won't work. You must walk away. Split! Say adios! This is not some cold mathematical calculus being used to determine our romantic lives. It is about the concept of enlightening oneself. It is about personal insight and going through the process of self-awareness, a process in which we rarely engage during our hormonally-charged youthful years.

Men and women are different by gender, have different plumbing and different chemistry that changes as we go through life. Many books have been written to illustrate the differences.

We'll never be 100 percent compatible. Maybe not 90 percent or even 80 percent. Throw in differences in our personalities, education, parental influences, experiences, and physical appearances and you can deduct another 10 to 40 percent. That means the chances of long-term compatibility can be 50 percent or less with each person you meet. No greater odds than flipping a coin, and that's even if you really, really like each other.

You may fall in love with many people, but unless you are committed to serial relationships you must determine your number and recognize that it will not be 100 percent. Perfection may be something to which you aspire, but it is the creator's domain.

When I accepted that each of us in the relationship has a special number and that neither of us were at 100 percent, I realized that I had to hone two additional skills to make my relationships last: the abilities to exercise tolerance and compassion.

It meant that I had to accept some things about another person that are nuances or represent behavioral tics that I have to tolerate and maybe even accept as part of what makes that person unique, adorable and lovable. It may seem like a crazy notion, and I am not boiling love down to a numerical value. It is, however, salient to accept that none of us is 100 percent. Not the cutest girl you've ever known. Not the smartest and sexiest gal you may have the pleasure to meet. Or the one at the top of her class or the best athlete in your circle of friends. I am telling you that even if you are a rare 90 to 95 percent and the two of you can't keep your hands off each other, your ideal mate will have to accept something about you that she would change if she could. It's a damn sobering reality.

My philosophy in regard to love—never give up hope—has been rewarded. Today I know that I am in love and that I do love. I have been captured by something so powerful that it has cemented my soul into a complete bond with another person. My partner, my life mate, and my love forever is Barbara. She is passionate and tender, firm but gentle, generous and selfless and replete with beauty and lust. She arouses the butterflies in my stomach and the yearning in my loins.

Within this bond I have discovered the importance of the patience I wasn't aware I possessed. Her pace is not always the same as mine. Her tastes are not always the same as mine. Her energy level is different. And yet we respect and tolerate those differences. Not only because we have developed compassion for each other, but we have evolved to the extent that each of us is able to accept that neither of us is 100 percent. We have accepted the differences that make each of us unique and interesting people. Her tolerance may waiver but never her loyalty. We do not waste time trying to change or fix each other. The acceptance is empowering, so much so that it has motivated me to become a better person. It has made it easy for me to contribute to and relish in Barbara's successes. The reward of her smile, a thank you, and a hug are more valuable than I ever imagined.

It may have taken a while to cultivate this aspect of life but I had a role model for the kind of nurturing, patience and tolerance that true love requires. I watched my father dress, feed, nurse and take care of my mother as her youthful figure, sharp mind, keen wit and personal independence ebbed during the years prior to her passing. Emphysema, caused by a lifetime of cigarettes, had summoned a sort of dementia that ended with a stroke just days before her seventy-first birthday. Whether Dad was acting out of a sense of responsibility due to her condition or a commitment due to the vows he had taken when he married my mother, I do not know. If he was compensating for the years she had tolerated his imperfections and nursed his arthritis, I do not know.

What I know beyond a doubt was that my father adored my mother. I know how sad he was after a life of hard work, making a home and raising a family, he was unable to spend his retirement years traveling and enjoying each day with the woman with whom he had shared life for fifty years. My father cherished my mother who was the only woman that had always been a rock in my life. During my mother's last years, he became a hero to me in ways that mattered more than anything else in my life. He loved my mother to the end and demonstrated to me patience, compassion and selflessness before which I had not known.

Since meeting Barbara, I can now say I have not only seen love, I have experienced it and I know what it is.

To you I say, "To know love, know your number and get over yourself."

Climate Fact:

Each week we ingest enough micro-plastic particles to make a credit card. Only 9% of plastic is recycled.

What can you do about it?

If you buy a plastic container for any purpose, you are responsible for being sure it is recycled. The same is true for cans and bottles.

If you don't recycle most things that come into your home, it's like throwing all of the trash onto your neighbor's lawn and then complaining about the pollutive eyesore it becomes.

Regrets

"Compassion is always in vogue."

Only one! There are things that could have fallen into this category if I had allowed them to exert too large a control over my life, but I didn't.

It is important to set goals. Sometimes I aimed for the far away planets but I came to understand that if I only made it to one in my own solar system I had accomplished something extraordinary. In other words, from time to time it has been necessary to acknowledge my progress and pat myself on the back. Positive self-feedback initiates a feeling of acceptance and for me and for most people, acceptance is euphoric.

I have acknowledged my failures, things one might call paths taken that didn't lead to the ultimate goal, but I wouldn't allow them to consume me or to define me. I prefer to call them temporary setbacks.

My father was really good at football but he got knocked down often. He convinced me that if that happened to me I had to get back up and keep playing. Those setbacks provided me with my greatest opportunities for learning. I have suffered, sometimes painfully, through an assortment of lessons presented by those opportunities, but I have never regretted the education they provided me.

What were the things that could have risen to the level of regret if I had allowed them to do that? The first is easy to mention. I wanted to be a star athlete. My father was a remarkable man. He was intellectually curious, well read, mechanically gifted, and athletically talented.

I was undersized and gifted with slow feet. I really wanted to be six-foot-five with large enough hands to play in the NBA. I had some talent, but I never found out what it was like to breathe the air above five-nine and one-half, dinky for the NBA. My height, nevertheless, has always been shorter than my ambitions. In spite of being shorter and slow, I was high point man, 22 points, in the off-campus championship game my senior year at Michigan. In my forties I played on teams that had back-to-back top three finishes at the Gus Macker Basketball Tournament, the largest "3 on 3 Basketball Tournament" on the planet. I was a basketball fanatic. I played until I was fifty years old when both my jump shot and my competitive urge for the game went south. We lost the off-campus championship game by two in overtime. That still irks me and the NBA went on without me. Neither is regrettable.

Just as much as I wanted to be a great athlete I wanted to be near the top of my class academically. Of 168 graduating seniors from my high school I finished in the 17th percentile.

No one ever shouted, "I finished 28th from the top," because it is far from academic perfection and flavored with disappointment. That degree and two years at a community college were good enough to earn me a scholarship offer from the University of Michigan. I accepted immediately for fear they might declare it a mistake, and I am still grateful they let me into their club. The Michigan business degree earned me a teaching fellowship that paid my tuition while I completed my MBA at Bowling Green.

The university was located in a small Ohio college town surrounded by endless fields of corn and soybeans. Unlike the academic rigor and politically active environment of the University of Michigan, Bowling Green was quiet, cautious and very white. The winters were brutal. The northern winds that blew across the flat farmlands were so frigid they cut me during hikes between campus buildings. During the two years I lived there I gained fifteen pounds and my jump shot went to hell.

In spite of those challenges, I left with another degree and two amazing children. Your mother and her brother were born while I attended the university. I may have started at twenty-eighth from the top but I was climbing, and I felt absolutely blessed to be Erica and Bradley's father. I wasn't yet aware that my marriage was unraveling so I had no regret at all.

My love for baseball made me yearn to be a statistician for the New York Yankees until a futile performance in a college statistics course soured me on that goal.

With an advanced business degree in hand I had the necessary tools for one who was destined to be his own boss and headed down a path where the need for calculus would be minimal. A hand-held calculator could take care of the math.

I still favor the Yankees, but when I attended the World Series game in Miami I rooted for the Florida Marlins. I was partying on Calle Ocho in Miami after Josh Beckett shut out the Yankees in game six to win the World Series in 2003.

During the previous off-season I had dined with most of the guys on that team so it had become as special a season for me as it must have been for them. I wasn't for a single moment jealous that someone else was crunching the numbers for the Bronx Bombers.

In my thirties I wanted to create a self-sufficient multi-family urban townhome as my residence. That would kick-start my path to financial independence. I would retrofit an old home and heat it with solar collectors. It would be a pioneering move, but I knew it would lower my monthly overhead. And, that would also allow me to do the kind of work that I liked and it could become a terrific home for my children.

The Oregon Historic District was a delightful place to live. The house I purchased there in 1976 was three stories of Federal style with ten-foot ceilings. It featured a large living room with a marble fireplace and a formal dining room that one entered through large French doors. The kitchen at the rear of the home was lined with solid oak cabinets that had the top doors removed to display restaurant ready bone-white china. I loved to cook and entertain. In the center of that spacious room sat a cooking island that would became party central in my grand scheme. Gatherings would be frequent and feature food, music, beer, herb and lots of laughter.

In that home my children could have their own bedrooms and enjoy comfortable surroundings in a trendy urban neighborhood. It spurred hopes that one or both would like to live with me, at least, part of the time. Their mother and I had divorced three years earlier. I got close to that aspiration: twenty-four hours close.

On the day before the closing on the mortgage loan for the three-unit building the solar-panel installer went belly-up and declared bankruptcy. That was in the early days of solar applications. The installer was under-financed and his supplier had slapped a mechanics lien on my house where his product was partially installed. I had failed to ask if his company was bonded to protect me from such an event. It was not.

Banks will not complete a mortgage loan if there is an active lien on the property. The time and money it took to overcome that setback changed the economics of the project and limited the time I would be able to reside in that home.

It was one of two major setbacks during those years. I was extremely disappointed that my plan for the home and a home for my children would have to be delayed. Although my time in that house was only five years, upon its completion in 1981, I became the first person in the United States to put 400 square feet of solar collectors on a multi-family residence listed on the National Register of Historic Places. And my children had a terrific second home for a while.

I recovered and developed a new goal. I wanted to make a six-figure income. There were more financially uncomfortable years in my life than I had anticipated, particularly during the years that Erica and Bradley were in school, but I persevered. I had to retrain and relocate but at the height of my business career I accomplished that goal. My walking around money grew to five figures every month. It led to travel and some financial security, but the money was never the ultimate goal. I just wanted to prove that I could do it. I think there were a lot of people counting upon me to do that much earlier in my life.

The world desperately needs to show more respect to people for whom money is not the sole purpose of their endeavors, but I had the tools to achieve financial success once I was able to place myself in the correct setting. In regard to money there is an old adage to which I subscribe: It's not how much you make. It's how much you keep. Regardless of how much money you make you must save part of it. Over time invest your savings in things that will grow. If you do this early in your life and maintain this discipline, you can become financially secure. I never achieved the status of wealthy or that place in life where you never ever worry about having enough money but I seldom lose sleep over it.

Here is another lofty ambition that didn't achieve the acclaim I sought. I wanted to write a novel that would inspire world peace. What was I thinking? With half of the people on the planet fighting over their religious preferences that was and still remains an illusory ideal.

Why was this important? During my life there has been so much war it made me yearn for the comfort that peace portends. There would be no such book penned by me, but after a collection of poetry and a few magazine articles I embarked upon a fast-paced ecological thriller.

The novel, although fictional, is based upon fact derived from four years of research and leads the reader on a romp from Tampa to Detroit with Derk Bryan, an EPA investigator, on the trail of a poison-peddling chemical company magnate. The bad guy, Jack Von Lleuwan, was a scratch golfer even with a patch over one eye and a gimp leg. He was teamed with a former pro-wrestler turned bodyguard who had anger management issues. I called the book Pest. Most of its readers were enlightened and entertained and once a year I get a tiny royalty check. Pest didn't change the world, but I am very proud of it. Upon its release, for a brief time in 2005 and 2006, the subject of Pest was the focus of various television and radio programs as I covered Florida during the book signing tour.

Pursuing goals is risky. It can lead to major frustration. Although insignificant in the scheme of human endeavors, one of the greatest challenges in my life I began pursuing in earnest in my sixties: golf.

Although I began playing golf in high school it wasn't until I took up residence on a golf course in 2006 that I decided to pursue a goal in golf. Golf is hard. Really hard, like waking to find that your dog has died and Donald Trump has become president. Furthermore, I lacked the two essential qualities for achieving excellence in golf: skill and temperament.

In spite of these inadequacies, I chose as my golf goal par for 72 holes. What was I thinking? I am trying to put a one-and-a-half-inch ball into a four-and-a-quarter-inch cup four hundred yards away. I'd have a better chance of getting to the Moon with only a jetpack strapped to my back.

Less than one tenth of one percent of golfers shoot par. Unlike all other sports, the ball just sits there, motionless, waiting to be hit. You have to make a miss-hit, an imperfect swing, an error in some way, not to hit the ball straight. And yet hitting the ball straight for any respectable distance in any consistent fashion is one of the most difficult things man has ever chosen to do.

It is physically demanding but the greater challenge of golf is the mental discipline it requires, especially if one's goal is par. That magic number called par, the number of strokes the designers of the game determined a golfer should take to get the ball from the tee into the cup on each hole, is elusive. It is the challenge I have chosen and the source of enormous pride and equally great frustration. The good news is I haven't thrown a club in months . . . well, I haven't hit anyone with a thrown club in months . . . and I am closing in on that magic number.

Why I invest so much emotional capital in such a silly game is probably due the culture in which I was raised. The messages I heard were clear: any job worth doing was worth doing well and when you work at something, work to win. When I reflect upon the reality that the average golfer has a difficult time breaking one hundred and, for a puny three weeks in 2016, my handicap dipped below ten, I regain my equilibrium. It's not life itself, just part of it, and I have chosen to accept the frustration along with the challenge. On any particular day I still don't know whether Jekyll or Hyde will tee off. I am competent at times and outrageously errant at others. What persists is what keeps any obsession alive: my commitment, my optimism, and my neurosis, so I practice and I compete.

Twice each week I play with a group of guys who throw $15-20 in a pot and attempt to earn it back on the golf course. The fact that

I end each year in the black suggests that I can hold my own, but my performance is far from dominating. During an average round I commit two to three balls to the depths of the local lakes. In the process I had two holes-in-one, a couple handfuls of eagles and a round of one over par. One time I scored one under par on the front nine but couldn't sustain it on the back. That round of eighteen holes in par seems both reachable and distant, but most would agree that a day on the golf course is better than a day in the office.

I get to spend hours with friends playing a game on exquisitely manicured environs that have become refuges for urban wildlife. Meanwhile people around the world are being repressed, shot at or herded into refugee camps. How could I have any regret about a golf score?

You may be noticing a trait in my behavior. I have lived most of my life trying to be above average, way above average. I have always wanted to be really good at not just some things but everything. I was affected by some highly-skilled people who instilled within me a penchant for achievement.

This drive in me was influenced by athletics and people like my father. He was a star athlete in high school with ambitions to play college football. He wasn't the only athlete in the family.

My cousin, Marvin Frey, earned a scholarship to play baseball at Michigan State University. He is a very successful dairy farmer.

Another cousin, Bruce Thompson, was the undeclared Valedictorian of his high school class and had the most deft jump shot I've ever seen, worth twenty points per game. He became a partner in a CPA firm.

His father and my uncle, Stanley Thompson, pitched a shutout and hit a home run to win the Michigan fast-pitch softball championship in his day. He formed a trio with Clark O'Donald and my father that played against teams from other small towns within driving distance of our home. That was until the other teams refused to play against them because that trio never lost.

Another cousin, Bill Myers, was elected vice-president of his class at Michigan State University and earned a Master's Degree in five years. He became the V.P. of International Marketing for Sylvania which was, at that time, a world-wide leader in lighting and television manufacturing. For a college graduation present his uncle gave him a shiny new red sports car.

I was driving a well-worn Ford Fairlane the day I left graduate school. These high achievers were part of my family as they are part of yours. They were role models for which average was not enough. We competed endlessly and whether we were engaged in checkers or Whiffleball winning became essential. It can be a heavy load to carry.

That's not a bad thing. Winning is happy stuff. Winning boosts my spirit. It will do the same for yours. Winning makes me fun to be around, confident but not arrogant. Losing makes me grumpy and sometimes ill-tempered. When I play even the simplest of games, I want to win, and when I win, I am happy. Losing is a bummer, a downer, and creates that 'Rats, I hate that!' kind of day. It's human nature to feel better after a success at anything, but I am unabashedly competitive about it.

The need to win has been a constant in my life, and I am satisfied with my achievements. On the other hand, the constant need to excel has been a burden to carry and sometimes a pain in the ass for those around me.

How so? I have little patience for sloppy ideas, lazy people or those who do not care if they succeed, like the people who do a job or play a sport while making it clear that they don't really care about the outcome. My impatience, I have been told, can be abrasive. I am more demanding of myself than of anyone else, but some have interpreted my emotional bursts of despair as negative expressions.

What they are witnessing is my burning desire to succeed. I do admit that controlling my emotions is part of that challenge of achievement.

The work ethic and integrity of my people compelled me to develop a set of principles by which to conduct my life. Gandhi taught me, "To be the world in which I want to live." My principles, my rigorous diet, my concern for environmental quality, and my sense of justice set a high bar for my life. Some have said it is too high, that I do not compromise or that I cling too stubbornly to my principles. I have had to accept that everyone will not be my friend, but most will respect me if my deeds match my words. The same is true for you.

Another aspect of this drive to achieve puts me into a continually active mode. I have worked hard and at a fast pace and I also seem in a hurry even when the goal is to relax. One can get a lot done like this, but it has been a challenge for those whom love me and desire that I share my time with them. Some of the people in my life about whom I care the most are still trying to hone my rough edges. For that I thank them.

I know I can't be the best at everything. No one can. Losing is part of life, and I have lost. I have lost competing in sports and in games. I have lost vying for love. I have had my setbacks in business from time to time. Life is a contact sport and you cannot go through it without some bruises. In fact, I have lost many times, but not nearly as often or as much as I have won. In spite of all that I have won and all that I have lost, I have no regrets about any of it. I am usually happy and often content.

So, what is my one regret? The one thing I would change if I could? The one regret, the big disappointment of my life, was the result of the separation from my children when your grandmother and I ended our marriage. My children, your mom and her brother, came to stay with me every other weekend whenever possible. We went on trips to visit their grandparents and took occasional vacations together. We went on weekend camping and skiing outings. We stayed in a beach house, gathered seashells and buried each other in the sand. We spent a lot of time partying with friends. We baked cookies and shaped them into funny faces. We did household chores, went to amusement parks, watched old black and white movies and munched on popcorn covered with nutritional yeast and kelp. I don't think they ever liked the popcorn like that, but they tolerated my healthy eating habits remarkably well. We went to soccer games, girl scout meetings, pottery classes and school events so I could hear their teachers praise them. We laughed a lot, cried sometimes and tried to understand each other. We didn't, however, live in the same house.

I cherished every minute of our time together, but sometimes I felt as if my children were just visitors in my life. Their real lives were lived elsewhere and I found myself feeling that my guidance, my rules and my ethics were not equal to the influence of their mother. I didn't despise her for that. She is a bright and caring mother with a wonderful sense of humor. I just wanted equal time and equal influence. Maybe I had that but it didn't feel that way to me. I dearly wanted them in my life.

Viewing my children today, one would say their lives are full. Nothing is missing. Thus, it turned out okay, whatever it was that their mother and I muddled through to provide. I would agree.

They are independent people who are competent, loyal, respected and liked by their friends and employers. They are smart, wry, and delightfully witty. They are interesting, honest and loving and can deliver criticism without fear. These are the people you would want in your life, and they are my children. On the day of my son's wedding, I saw my daughter and my son dancing with people who had discovered these qualities in them and deeply loved them for it.

It was a day that filled me with pride like no other in my life. So yes, I think they turned out okay. Stunningly, splendidly okay. We all did.

Of course, the divorce exacted a toll on each of us. Change that momentous always does. It confused us and sometimes fractured us. It led to my only real regret. I missed hearing my children's stories each day upon their return from school. I missed seeing their smiles and hearing them laugh. I missed drying their tears, mending their wounds and soothing their souls when things didn't go so well. I missed helping with homework. I missed shopping for shoes with them. I missed tucking them into their beds each night, reading to them and assuring them that tomorrow would be a glorious day to be alive. I missed that one-on-one, close-up and personal experience of being the father in their lives every single day.

How did I cope? Not always well, but I eventually adopted the perspective that being a parent is like running a marathon. It's a long-distance event. Once a parent, always a parent. In spite of the separation from the daily lives of my children, I looked upon that segment of our lives as just that, one segment. They and I would be around for a long time, and their childhood was to be only one part of our lives together.

Operating on that premise got me through the difficult times, but it didn't make me happy. I was still angry that the breakdown of my marriage had led to the breakdown of my family. I didn't want to live apart from my children, and I had to miss the most significant part of being a parent: just being there.

Their mother was disappointed, too, but for different reasons. Neither of us had gotten our needs met and we were either too immature, too stubborn or just too different to do anything about it. I was angry that I had to live without my children. She had to go on with her life under circumstances that she wished were different or better. As a result, there were times she expressed to me doubt about how good a mother she was. I assured her then and can tell you that your terrific grandmother was a terrific mother, too.

Fortunately, I had parents who nurtured my optimistic mindset and instilled within me the notion that all things are possible. I would not allow disappointment, or setback of any kind, to define my life. The divorce would be just one episode in my life. As a regret that one has passed as did my children's youth.

My viewpoint today is that my life has been blessed. I have done important work and have tried to leave a small carbon footprint while doing so. I have traveled far and made many friends. My children have grown to become affable and loving people with productive lives. I respect and love them today more than ever.

It is easy to have regrets. With life comes disappointment. But life is precious, and it is short. The earth is four and one-half billion years old. If we live on it for one hundred years, that is but a speck of dust in time.

This one life, of yours and of mine, is it. Once chance. One dance. Go for it! Conceive it, believe it, achieve it and have no regrets.

Climate Fact:

The largest banks in the United States continue to finance fossil fuel exploitation, production and distribution at record levels.

What can you do about it?

Money talks! Put your money somewhere else. Choose money market accounts or small local banks that do not lend to fossil fuel producers.

Time is on your side

"The worst kind of information to have is the stuff you know for sure that ain't so."

Would you rather have a million dollars today or one cent doubled each day for a month?

A junior high school classmate asked me that question one day. He was no mathematics genius, and the answer seemed obvious. Those days it cost a buck to go to a movie so a million dollars was huge, and one cent seemed skimpy in comparison even if doubled each day forever. In my opinion it was a no-brainer, but I hadn't done the math. Nor had I learned the impact of time upon compound interest. I was only eleven years old.

Why is this so important to understand? Your concept of time and your use of time will shape your future. Some say there isn't enough time to get done what they want to do each day. They're common complaint is, "I never have enough time." Others say, "Time heals all wounds."

On the subject of time I agree with the Rolling Stones. In a song by the same name they made it clear when they said: "Time is on my side. Yes it is."

At age ten you are not yet aware that the Rolling Stones may be the greatest rock 'n roll band of all time, but that is another subject. Why do I agree with them that time is on your side?

The concept of time has become essential in helping us navigate daily life, place important events into perspective, and process financial transactions. Most people on this planet use the Gregorian calendar in which each day consists of approximately twenty hours. Leap years have been added to adjust for the differences between the 24-hour clock and the actual time it takes for a single rotation of the Earth. We've been using this system and its predecessor for two thousand years.

This calendar is crucial to our lives. You'll probably never meet someone who cannot tell you his or her birth date. Most of us work a fixed number of hours each day and each week and look forward to the rest of the time to spend with friends, families and engage in our hobbies. We plan vacations and family get-togethers based upon holidays that occur on the same date each year. If the sun is rising in the sky we know that it must be close to seven a.m. and if it is setting it must be six or seven or eight p.m. depending upon the time of year. Astrophysicists know that if one travels fast enough, time can bend back upon itself. In essence we can go backward in time. It is unlikely we shall ever experience this phenomenon, but what these same scientists have demonstrated is that time is artificial. It is a creation of man and a very useful one as I shall explain.

If I offer you nothing more than an understanding of the power of large numbers and impact that time can have upon them I feel I have been an attribute to your life.

This was my experience. In my forties, much later than I should have begun, I started saving a few dollars each month. Each time I got paid, before I spent any of my paycheck on beer, food, rent or anything else, I put twenty-five dollars into an investment account called an IRA, an Individual Retirement Account. I had the money automatically drawn from my checking account and placed into a large mutual fund where the money was combined with other people's money and invested in American enterprises. Americans are many things but we are first and foremost capitalists, and we are the best in the world at it. The primary scorekeeper for this part of our lives is the New York Stock Exchange. Since its inception the New York Stock Exchange and the capital markets in our great country have returned an average of seven percent per year on the money invested in them. There have been up years and down years, recessions and even a Great Depression, but we have survived and prospered.

Through the political debates regarding tax codes, regulations and all the other parameters of commerce our economic system has produced wealth for those whom have been keen enough to appreciate the opportunity it presents.

As the stock markets went up and down during my life one thing never changed, my confidence in American capitalism and my commitment. Each month and each year I added to my IRA. As my income grew the amount of savings I put into this investment account increased because I had a religious-like faith in two impelling truths: 1. Always bet on America and 2. Listen to the Rolling Stones.

The Dow Jones Industrial average has been a durable performance indicator of our stock market. On December 31, 1976 the Dow stood at 1005. I put my first twenty-five dollars in an IRA in 1986. Thirty years later, on December 31, 2016, the Dow Jones was approaching 20,000. That means that a dollar invested in 1977 would have been worth about twenty dollars forty years later. I only wish I had begun the routine ten years earlier.

What is at work here is the impact of compound interest on regular savings and investment over time. Small amounts invested regularly become large over time as the interest, dividends and earnings from them are accrued and reinvested. For example, if you save $50 each month at the average seven percent rate of return of the U.S. stock market, you will have $120,000 after forty years. A

$200 per month savings could grow to $500,000 and by investing $400 per month the pie could grow to a million dollars.

The price of a movie ticket is now about eight dollars with my senior discount, but a million dollars is still a bloody fortune to most of the people on this planet. Four hundred dollars may seem like a lot of money to a ten-year-old but it will not be out of reach when you complete your education and begin working. Do not forget the impact of time upon large numbers. Save, invest and you can become a millionaire.

Why is money so important? You cannot become fifteen years old, forty years old or ninety years old without living all of the years before those birthdays. If your goal is to live to be one hundred, as is mine, you are now aware that it is possible to save enough money by your sixties to do whatever you want for the rest of your life. The freedom this can bring you, the quest of which is an essential part of our nature if your last name is Myers, is empowering.

Imagine what you can accomplish by achieving this financial security. You could pursue a hobby, travel the world, and/or create things that help make the world a better place for all of mankind. In the process you will have succeeded with the first order of being a person on this planet: you have taken care of yourself. It is important to take care of yourself, not only due to the opportunities this provides, but so you do not become a burden to others.

Life is filled with challenges. There will be ups and downs. As a society we must accept that there are times when people need a safety net and we should provide it, but we are first and foremost responsible for taking care of ourselves. Developing financially responsible habits is as important to your wellbeing and longevity as exercising and avoiding junk food and pesticides in your diet. You should act as if the quality of your life depends upon it because it does.

I wish I had begun building the kind of nest-egg I have described for you in my twenties instead of my forties. Nevertheless, by applying these simple principles I was able to create a supplemental income for my retirement years that I can depend upon for the rest of my life.

By the way, when I got around to doing the math on a penny doubled each day for a full month, the total exceeded ten million dollars on the 31st day of the month.

Now I can you hear singing along with the Rolling Stones, "Time is on my side, yes, it is."

Climate Fact:

The wealthiest 10% among us are responsible for 50% of greenhouse gas pollution. They live in over-sized houses, drive oversized cars and buy stuff they don't need. The poorest 50% produce only 12% of GNG.

What can you do about it?

Strive for whatever makes you happy but remember that every decision you make either adds to the problem or becomes part of the solution. We are all in this together.

Planes, Trains and Cruise Ships

"Humans have succeeded extravagantly at the expense of
other species."

Cruise ships provide us with an opportunity to see places otherwise out of reach for the average person. There are cruises for families, seniors, gays, jazz lovers and more. I prefer long boats that sail rivers with a view of the shore. Recently I made an exception and boarded a cruise ship with Barbara to sail around the south coast of Spain. Stops were planned for ports from Sevilla to Barcelona.

When I arrived at my stateroom six plastic bottles of water were neatly stacked on a shelf. When I left the ship for shore excursions I was encouraged to take bottled water with me. Cruise ships are noted for their hospitality, and everyone knows it's important to stay hydrated, so this was a nice touch. Cruise ships are also noted for food. From buffets to lounge bars and poolside cafes to fine dining restaurants, every food option is available. At each meal or snack, beer, wine and soft-drinks are available in a bottle.

Ever the environmentalist, I got to wondering what they did with all the empty containers. With cruise ships now transporting the population of small towns, the waste is enormous. I would be troubled to find that my desire to travel was adding to the pollution that was igniting global temperatures.

How much pollution and waste? Our ship, the Pursuit by Azamara, sailed with 664 passengers and a crew of over 300. The

Icon, by Royal Caribbean, carries 10000 passengers plus crew. It releases four times the amount of CO2 into the atmosphere per person than flying and staying in a four-star hotel. One cruise ship can release as much CO2 as a million cars. One study revealed that the 218 cruise ships in Europe released four times more sulfur oxide than all of the cars in Europe. Cruise ships comprise only 1% of the world's fleet, but they create 25% of the waste in the ocean. This is huge problem for a world needing to reduce the use of fossil fuels.

I dialed the front desk and was pleased to discover that an Environmental Officer is now required on cruise ships in Europe. Duarte, an articulate man of Polish descent in his fifties, was happy to meet with me and show me what they did with all those plastic and glass bottles. I was pleased to find that the captain can lose his license for failing to abide by the environmental regulations so the captain listens to the Environmental Officer. Duarte also said that regulations in Europe are much stricter than those in the United States.

So, what becomes of the thousands of containers that would otherwise clog landfills and end up in our air, water and soil? Duarte took us to a room below deck where they smash them into pieces or crush them flat. All of the glass bottles used on the Pursuit in one week can be crushed into boxes that make up only 3-4 cubic feet. The plastic bottles are squished into a box the size of 1 ½ cubic feet. They are off loaded at each port in recyclable cardboard boxes. From there they can be sent to recycling facilities by the local port officials. Food wastes are finely chopped and discarded, at least, 12 miles from shore. Human waste is processed by non-aerobic digesters and treated before being discharged. All of this is good, but not standard practice by all cruise ships.

We flew to Europe. Airplanes are responsible for 9% of carbon emissions but far less than cruise ships. Although cruising for 7 days is three times more carbon intensive than flying and staying in a hotel, there is good news. By 2030 European cruise ships will be required to hook up to electric outlets when in port to reduce emissions from diesel fuels and Liquid Natural Gas that is often used while at sea. The Pursuit burns low sulfur oil inside 12 miles from port and heavy oil outside, but it recycles the exhaust to heat boilers to keep carbon emissions to a minimum. In the works are fuel cells and battery propulsion.

Railroads emit 80% less carbon emissions than truck and ships. Although I drive an electric car, we took the train to and from my home in Boynton Beach to the Miami Airport. In Portugal the train took us from Porto to Lisbon, in comfort, where we boarded the Pursuit.

Next time you plan a trip think about your carbon footprint and leave the old gas guzzler in the garage.

Climate Fact:

Surveys of young people indicate that over 50% are worried about the effects of global warming upon their future.

What can you do about it?

You should be. We really messed up. However, the future is not ordained. It is in your hands. Take action. Make wise choices. Become a model for others.

Letting go

*"If you are in harmony with the laws of the universe you
will be in harmony with what we often call God."*

"Ring. Ring. Ring. Ring!"

It was early in May when the phone disrupted a training session
I was conducting for two sales reps in my Miami home.

I had relocated my life and my business to a 1950's home located
two blocks from Brickell Avenue near the financial district. My
business was spinning off a six-figure income and I was re-investing
in urban condos and single-family homes.

My object had been to find one of the worst homes in a
neighborhood with rising appeal and appreciating value. My father,
the contractor, had exposed me to enough building construction that
all I had to do was fit one of those rundown old homes into the
financial model I had developed. Then I would renovate it.
Sometimes I would live in it during the process.

I began flipping residences for huge gains and reinvesting in
rentals for long term cash flow. I finished off the remodel by installing
a back yard putting green and a hot tub under the canopy of a
magnificent Poinciana Tree. I had created a tropical paradise in the
city, i.e., if you didn't mind the sound of an occasional jet passing
overhead. I really liked that home but knew I had to move on.

Since 2001, when I purchased that property, I had watched the housing market approach bubble status with the knowledge that this home would play a major role in my retirement plan. The realization that I was in my mid-fifties with twenty-eight years left on my mortgage provided another motivator for moving. As my own boss I had no one contributing to my retirement program so I had to become comfortable with the disruption caused by periodic relocation. I had read about successful people's willingness to go where the opportunities resided. It may have been a rationalization but it made me feel better about leaving.

I have moved twenty-five times in my life which is about once every three years. In the process my closest friends and family became scattered, and I miss them. I didn't meld into the Latin culture of Miami, but I was otherwise content in that place.

The phone rang again. "This is Spencer. May I help you?" I answered in my business voice.

Some calls can change one's life. This was one of those.

The person on the telephone told me that my father's car had been struck by a drunken driver. He had been taken to a hospital in northern Michigan. Other than being told that one of my children had been injured I couldn't have received worse news.

My mother had died a few years earlier and it had been a painful experience for me. I was not ready to lose my father. Since then Dad had developed a wonderful relationship with a former high school classmate that took him on excursions all over the country. Cybil, a girl he had always liked while in school, became his new traveling companion. She was particularly fond of casinos, and their car was T-boned at an intersection on their way to a casino near Cadillac, Michigan. Although they remained in their own homes thirty minutes apart they spent most of their free time together. I was so happy Dad had found a comfortable match with whom to spend his remaining years, a time he had always expected to live out with the love of his life, my mother. The only unusual aspect of their relationship was his willingness to attend the casinos. That seemed out of character for a guy who told me when I was age eight years old, after giving me some money to attend the county fair and its games of chance, "Gamble only what you can afford to lose." That was then and never has been much.

The gloom deepened when my sister, Gretchen Myers, told me that he was not conscious and suggested he might not awaken. A sinking feeling in my gut, like a free fall in a roller coaster, gripped me. I was physically shaken by the prospect of losing him. Dad and I had become much closer since Mother's passing. We talked regularly and he frequently visited me in Florida, a place he had disdained for most of his life due to the heat and the political persuasion of southern whites. I postponed the training and reserved a next day flight to Grand Rapids along with a rental car that would take me to Traverse City.

In the hospital I held his hand while he lay motionless. I talked to him as if he were fully alert. There was no pouring out of heart due to a fear that some things would never be said nor was there any attempt to reveal some emotion that had not been expressed between us.

I knew that he loved me and that I was a source of great pride to him. I was equally proud to call him my father. That day I was there to bring him through what no medical procedure could hope to accomplish. He was in a coma from which he was unlikely to recover.

I tried my best to maintain a sense of humor, something all of the Myers' family used not only to diffuse deeply emotional moments but also to connect with each other. It was never easy for either of us to tell the other, "I love you." I'm not sure that I told him on that occasion because we expressed that through laughter, loyalty, working together, sports, games and family activities.

It took me a long time but I learned from my mother that I had to ask for it. I can barely describe, though, how wonderful it felt when I finally heard him say to me, "I love you." It had taken him a long time to do that.

It took me as long to learn that he needed the same from me. The moment I was able to force out, "I love you, Dad," his leathery shield softened. He changed. We both changed.

The major catalysts for that evolution were the hugs he got from his grandchildren. With each embrace I could sense his inner child glowing. His grandchildren did what the rest of us tried to do for years. They got him to be a hugger.

My father was very physical and liked contact sports, particularly football.

That's likely why he spent hours wrestling and playing with me like a lion cub when I was a child. He wasn't a hugger, though, and long before junior high school began I had less and less physical contact with him. I missed that.

Eventually, all of the hugs his grandchildren gave him melted his resistance and the teddy bear in him emerged. It was quite a transformation for someone conditioned to suppress his emotions.

Although my father wasn't an emotionally articulate guy he displayed enormous love. He may not have been the best spouse one could have had but he was devoted as spouse, a father, a teacher and a man guided by the kind of principles anyone could use to answer a fundamental question, "Am I a good person?"

My father represented the best in our country. He thought that marriage was about two people sharing their lives together to create and nourish a family and each had to fully contribute. Even though they had their conflicts he cherished my mother and was a dedicated father. I may have had an advantage over my sister simply because I was a man. Dad could communicate with other men. I believe that it was much more difficult for him with women, and that may be another trait we have inherited from him.

He also thought that each of us was responsible for taking care of ourselves so he valued self-sufficiency. Everyone deserved an opportunity to succeed so he railed against discrimination of any kind. He served with people of color during the war and felt that rampant racial discrimination was not only morally repulsive but it shortchanged our country's potential. Although he had grown up in an all-white town, when the racial riots ravaged many inner cities in the sixties he told me, "If this nation is going to ask black men and women to fight for it, then it has to treat them better."

He held a generally favorable view about the benefit of unions and was responsible for forming one in a company for which he had worked for several years. Firsthand experience, however, had taught him that rank and file union members too often made unenlightened and unreasonable demands. His philosophy was that workers and companies prospered if they worked in the best interests of all parties. He regularly disdained supervisory positions in the carpenters union because it would pit him against his fellow workers. Too often that would require him to plead the corporate point of view when it was not a just one. He was a man of stubborn principle ruled by fairness and justice.

After contracting rheumatoid arthritis at age forty-eight he was unable to sustain a fulltime job so he built a rental property for horse lovers on a five-acre plot next to his home, completely from recycled materials. He then opened a shoe and leather repair business in his garage and planted hundreds of fir trees that he eventually sold during the holidays for many years. He increased the value of his twenty-acre country homestead over fifty times its purchase price.

He had a keen eye for things that were under-valued and how to magnify their worth.

He paid homage to God and was once a member of the Episcopal Church. He had us baptized there. I think he was guided more by the principles set forth in Ten Commandments and I know he favored the food and wine they served at their deistic conventions over the fellowship of evangelicals. One time he said to my sister, Gretchen, who had become overzealous in her bible studies, "Leave it outside." Dad despised hypocrites.

My father was a self-styled man, an avid reader and an inventor, but his desire for independence and privacy guided him. For example, from old parts he constructed an apple cider press on his property that would allow people with apple trees to turn them into cider for a processing fee of fifty cents per gallon. He wanted to help people with fruit trees in their yards benefit from that.

He came up with practical solutions for simple problems. When I did a back-of-the-envelope calculation that projected a profit of twenty thousand dollars during the two-month-long season, he pressed another forty gallons and dismantled his nascent enterprise. I was dumbfounded until he reflected, "I don't want all those people in my backyard."

Another time he built lightweight portable shanties that could easily be dragged onto the ice and set up by one man. They provided protection from the cold Michigan winters for folks who loved to fish through the ice. My cousin, Norman Frey, described my father's abilities as, "Pure genius."

When I suggested that he sell the plans for the shanties through ads in wildlife magazines he wasn't the least bit interested. He was just trying to make one of his favorite past-times more enjoyable for his friends and family.

I think that Dad voted for Democrats most often but he was dismayed when the Dixie-crats became Republicans after the passage of federal civil rights and voting registration laws in the 1960s. He considered that transformation indicative of southern white bigotry and the most blatant and powerful force to promote racism in the U.S.–use of the ballot box.

My father was as honest as Abe and he expected everyone else to be that way. If you lied to him you quickly used up your goodwill. His honesty and sense of fair play emanated from a set of morale principles that characterized a man of immense integrity. What best illuminated Dad's integrity was a statement by the minister at his memorial service in 2002.

"I didn't always agree with George's politics but if something were to happen to me I would want George Myers to raise my son." It would be difficult for anyone to rate a higher honor.

About my father I say to you, "It would not be a mistake to emulate him, but whatever you become in your life, be a hugger."

Climate Fact:

More than 8 million registered voters in the U.S. who have indicated that environmental issues are their number one concern did not vote in the last presidential election.

What can you do about it?

Contact your elected representatives and let them know what you want to be done. Vote for change.

Inspiration

At age seventy-nine I have realized that, among many things, I am no longer hip, cool, neat or whatever term is being applied today to people who are consummate texters, tweeters, Skypers or Facebook junkies. I am no longer part of the "in crowd."

I haven't memorized or perfected the myriad abbreviations used in place of real language on every sort of wireless device. Thx, idk and lol are just incomplete spellings to me. For the ultimately literate, these may represent a step backward, a loss of our communication skills and a fraying of the fabric that knits us together as a humanity.

The world has changed from that of our ancestors and it is changing again. One may not always like change but it is inevitable. Generations before us have lamented change with despair. It comes too fast, they say. When I was a child we used a slide rule for mathematic calculations. Today you have a computer in your pocket more powerful than the one used in the first space ship. When I was in high school having a child out of wedlock could tie a social albatross around your neck. Today people of the same gender may marry each other.

Change is often difficult, but I am optimistic. You should be, too. I am not fearful of change. I am sometimes concerned and sometimes mystified by the degree and pace of change, but most of the time I am encouraged by it. I choose to be optimistic because I am a member a family, the human family, that has the capacity to adapt and to grow with each and every change we encounter in our lives.

This is important because we are now in the midst of a change in the culture of man as significant as we experienced during the Industrial Revolution. This is occurring simultaneously with the existential threat of global warming. The stakes for humanity could not be higher. Technological advances in communications and medicine along with changes in our sources and uses of energy have already transformed our habits, customs, economics, politics, and personal and international relationships in new and exciting ways. The climate crisis demands even more radical change and adaptation to the unfamiliar and potentially uncomfortable. Whether we drive the cars or the automobiles drive us, the future will be filled with change and challenges, but it will be a great time to be alive.

I am optimistic because our need to be free will be met with an expansion of our ability to express it. Our sensitivity to the planet that is our home will be met with new ways to sustain it. Our cultures will intermix with greater frequency as our economies become interdependent and our communications instant. The world can be an oyster for more and more people.

At the same time, there will continue to be people who are doubters, those who will attempt to restrict our freedoms due to their own insecurities, and those who will stand against this march of humanity because they assume it somehow benefits them. One of my favorite teachers once told me: "The only things in life that are certain are death and taxes." To that I add change. Change is inevitable.

There is positive news here. As a member of this family you have been blessed with the ability to negotiate with and prosper from these changes.

My father once told me during a hunting trip, "Stand on the hill by this tree and everything will ultimately pass you." He may not have been referring to the old Chinese adage about time, but the doubters and the intolerant will ultimately be washed away by time's inevitable passage. They will change, too, and life will go on.

It is my hope that you will be living, breathing and experiencing this rare gift called life with some of the zest and imagination that has been passed unto us by our ancestors and by the bounty of this special place we call Earth. And as you go forth into the world you can be proud of your heritage and your accomplishments.

Climate Fact:

Greta Thunberg was only 16 years old when she appeared before a gathering of the United Nations. In essence she said that Climate Change is short changing her generation.

What can you do about it?

Every decision you make from here on will either feed or defeat the enemy.

About the Author

G. Spencer Myers' specialty is the eco-political thriller, featuring Dr. Derk Bryan, college professor, obsessive environmentalist and intrepid EPA investigator who works only on cases involving environmental chaos and dead bodies. His blogs feature controversial issues from an ecological point of view.

His first book, Pest, featured a race against the clock to save his former girlfriend from a fraudulent pesticide manufacturer and an ex-wrestler turned body guard with anger management issues. In Dead Wrong he exposes the link between a toxic spill, police corruption and a Johnny Cash look alike. His memoir, A Letter to My Grandson, inspired the 1st Palm Beach County Short Story Contest entitled, "In Search of Integrity."

In The Girl with the Red Nails, the antagonist is Pendleton Danswirth III, but the real villain is plastics. Since its completion the EPA has chosen to regulate so called forever chemicals in drinking water. His recent article on sustainable cruising has appeared in newspapers throughout Florida under The Invading Seas series.

Constantly striving to reduce his own carbon footprint, in 1980 he became the first person in the U.S. to put solar panels on a multi-family home listed on the National Register of Historic Places. He refuses to live in a home without a south facing roof.

Mr. Myers is a graduate of the University of Michigan, holds an MBA from Bowling Green State University and is Certified by the American College of Sports Medicine.

He is a native of Michigan but lives in Boynton Beach, FL where he is still in pursuit of par. Contact him at Author@GSpencerMyers.com.